Chapter 1

Sunday, July 10, 1898
Hartford, Connecticut

Concordia Wells hesitated in the foyer of the Ladies' Restaurant in Brown Thomson's department store, knowing she only delayed the inevitable.

She tugged at her gloves and eyed the crowded dining room, finally catching sight of the primly postured lady in dove gray at a corner table. Her mother's heart-shaped face, china-blue eyes, and blond hair – fading now to silver – had made her a beauty in her prime. Concordia had grown up wishing she had inherited her mother's looks, instead of the unfortunate freckled complexion, red hair, and petite stature of her father's Scottish ancestors.

As she approached, her mother inclined her head in polite greeting.

That was promising. At least she was not scowling. Concordia recalled the sharp words that had accompanied the scowl last week.

A transcontinental trip aboard a sleeper train! How safe are these machines, hurtling toward the opposite end of the country with such unseemly haste?

Your reputation and your purse will most certainly be at risk. I have heard that confidence men engage in nomadic flirtations aboard trains, in order to steal both.

Teaching at a women's college has made you bold. It is high time you marry David and settle down.

Concordia stifled a sigh. With her mother, every issue came back to marriage.

She had an urgent reason for leaving Hartford, as her mother well knew. What more was there to discuss?

The waiter brought over a plate of dainty viands: egg-salad on thinly sliced bread, sponge cakes, and mouth-watering scones with raspberry jam. When he was gone, her mother plucked a sugar cube with delicate tongs. "Are you all packed for tomorrow?"

Concordia nodded.

"I would like to accompany you as far as New York," her mother said.

"Why?"

Her mother frowned. "It is far safer and more decorous for a young lady to travel with a proper chaperone."

"It is a short trip between Hartford and New York," Concordia said.

Her mother dropped her voice to a conspiratorial whisper. "I worry about the Inner Circle. You should not travel alone."

Concordia busied herself with applying jam to a scone, hoping her mother would not notice her trembling hands.

The Inner Circle. She tried to hide the shudder that ran through her at the reminder of the powerful group responsible for the events of a few months before. Even though disbanded and many of its members brought to justice, a few remained unnamed, the only witnesses forever silenced. She, Penelope Hamilton, and Lieutenant Capshaw of the Hartford Police had been responsible for discovering and thwarting the Circle's bold plot last May.

Her own involvement had not been without consequences. She thought of the shadowy figure who lingered near her mother's home at dusk almost every summer evening these past few weeks, slipping away before the police could confront him and learn his business.

Finally she looked up. Her mother was watching her with anxious eyes. Concordia gave the most reassuring smile she could manage. "I will be glad for your company."

"I should also like to see Miss Hamilton again," her mother said.

Concordia raised an eyebrow. "You want her assurances that I will be properly monitored, don't you?"

It was fortunate that, despite the events of the past few months, her mother was unaware of Penelope Hamilton's work as a Pinkerton detective, or of the undercover assignment behind their upcoming cross-country trip. Such information might require the application of smelling salts.

Concordia smiled to herself. She had met Penelope two years before, during her first semester of teaching at Hartford Women's College. Penelope at the time was the school's lady principal – a position second to the college's president in terms of prestige and responsibility. Only a select few on the board of trustees had known that Lady Principal Hamilton was to investigate the financial mismanagement going on at the college. Concordia had stumbled upon the lady principal's secret and had been of some help with the case. The two had been friends ever since.

"When you have children of your own, you will understand these things," her mother said, breaking into her thoughts.

Concordia threw up her hands. "At least you are no longer raising objections to the trip itself."

Her mother cleared her throat. "Actually, I need you to do something for me while you are in San Francisco."

Ah, so that was it. Concordia smiled behind her teacup.

"Do you remember your Aunt Estella and her husband Karl?" her mother asked, inclining her head politely across the dining room, toward a group of ladies from her bridge club. Though her facial expression seemed relaxed, Concordia noted the thin hands keeping a white-knuckled grip on the spoon as she stirred her tea.

Concordia narrowed her eyes. What was wrong here? She tried to recall her mother's youngest sister, but the memories were dim. Aunt Estella – or Stella, as she preferred – had moved to California with her husband shortly after they married, more than a dozen years ago. Correspondence had been infrequent over the years, and her aunt had never returned to the area for a visit.

"They have a little girl now, do they not?" Concordia asked.

"Two girls," her mother corrected. "Ten and four years old."

It had been longer than she thought. "Do you want me pay them a visit, and bring a gift of some kind?"

Her mother hesitated.

"Has something happened?" Concordia's voice rose of its own accord.

Her mother glanced uneasily at the heads swiveling toward their table. She made a discreet *shushing* gesture. "A bit quieter, if you please." She passed a slip of paper over the jam pot. "I received an alarming telegram from Estella yesterday."

At the sight of the words on the page, a stirring of unease inched up Concordia's spine. KARL HAS DISAPPEARED WITHOUT WORD. CAN YOU COME? AM FRANTIC. STELLA.

"Disappeared? What do you think has happened?" Concordia asked.

Her mother blotted her lips with a napkin. "Estella's last letter described Karl as oddly secretive recently. He's been bringing home more money than usual, too. You may remember that your aunt is a bit…well, flighty, shall we say…so for her to notice that something is amiss…." Her voice trailed off.

"There's more, isn't there?" Concordia said.

Her mother glanced at the napkin in her lap, now twisted in restless hands. "I fear he may have fallen in with bad company again."

"Again?"

"Before he met my sister, Karl Brandt was in trouble with the law. I don't know exactly what he did."

Her mother's neutral expression could not quite conceal the pain and embarrassment in her eyes. Not wanting to cause further distress, Concordia kept her response noncommittal. "I was unaware of his…background."

"Naturally, one does not widely disseminate such information." Her mother shifted uneasily. "It is an awkward subject."

"Why would Estella marry someone like that?" Concordia asked.

Her mother sighed. "He was a handsome, charming man in his younger days, and she was quite enamored of him."

Concordia raised an eyebrow. Such characteristics could easily describe any number of confidence men who left penniless or bigamous wives in their wake, though not after twelve years. "No one intervened to stop such a union?"

Her mother grimaced. "She's the younger child of the family, and rather spoiled. She always got her way."

Perhaps that was why Mother had been so strict with her and her sister Mary, Concordia reflected. She wondered what Aunt Stella was like now, with children of her own to raise. Perhaps motherhood had brought about more maturity? That was certainly true for Concordia, who had become a surrogate mother of sorts to the two dozen college girls she lived with during the school year. Their well-being was solely her responsibility, and she found herself sounding like Mother all too often.

She handed back the telegram. "What do you want me to do?"

"I certainly don't want you to try to find him. Heaven knows you have had more than your share of trouble with unscrupulous people." Her mother's clear blue eyes narrowed in disapproval.

Concordia resisted the impulse to argue the point. She certainly did not *seek out* such trouble, though there was no denying her involvement in several unpleasant incidents in recent years.

"The police can search for Karl," her mother went on. "I merely want you to talk with Estella, convince her to return to Hartford with her girls. They can stay with me for a while." She slid an envelope across the table. "This should be sufficient train fare for them to accompany you back. The address is in there, too. I will inform her you intend to visit."

Concordia tucked the envelope into her purse. "I'll be happy to speak with her, but what if she refuses to leave?"

Her mother blinked back tears. "I pray you can persuade her. Heaven help them if they stay."

Chapter 2

Monday, July 11, 1898
Hartford, Connecticut

David Bradley accompanied Concordia and her mother to Union Depot the next morning. Her fiancé appeared quite dapper today, attired in high summer style. Gone were his customary professorial spectacles and rumpled houndstooth coat, replaced by a light seersucker jacket of navy blue that fit smoothly over his broad shoulders. She resisted the urge to reach over and stroke the dark hair curling at the nape of his neck, beneath the jaunty straw boater hat. *Mercy.* Betrothed or not, that simply would not do.

They climbed to the railway platform, where a gaunt, stoop-shouldered policeman waited.

"Lieutenant Capshaw! This is a surprise," Concordia said.

She had first met Aaron Capshaw two years ago, when he was investigating the sudden death of a staff member at Hartford Women's College, along with a string of other disturbing incidents at the school. She had been of some assistance to the police at the time, though Capshaw referred to it as *meddling.* Since then, circumstances had brought her and Capshaw together on other cases. In the midst of one of them, Concordia's best friend Sophia Adams and the lieutenant had fallen in love. To Concordia's delight, they had married last year. She was happy to call Capshaw a friend.

Before this, Concordia would have been astounded at the idea of being on such easy terms with a policeman, of all people – women of her social station hardly interacted with such persons on a regular basis. Despite their friendship, it seemed awkward calling Capshaw by his Christian name. She knew he felt the same about her.

As she gazed upon the tall, thin figure with red hair brighter than her own, she noted the tension in his jaw and realized his presence shouldn't surprise her. He was working on the Inner Circle case, after all.

"I'm making sure you get aboard safely, miss," Capshaw said. He glanced uneasily up and down the platform.

A tingle of fear rippled through her. She leaned in and whispered, "No progress in locating the remaining members?"

He shrugged. "We have some leads, but it's just as well you're leaving town. So long as you stay out of trouble on this trip," he added sternly.

Concordia kept her voice low, as her mother and David were in conversation only a few feet away. "Penelope is the one on assignment, not I."

"That may well be," he said. "But it has never stopped you before. I don't want to get a telegram about you stumbling upon a body, or some such mischief." His newly grown-in mustache – he had shaved it months before when he had gone into hiding – twitched in a suppressed smile. Concordia could almost hear the policeman's oft-muttered words: *meddling females*. Well, she intended to stay out of trouble this time. She was to be Penelope's companion, nothing more.

Her mother approached and handed her valise to Capshaw. "Would you mind helping me find a porter, lieutenant?" She cast a knowing look at David and her daughter. "We'll give these two a chance to say a proper goodbye."

Concordia's cheeks grew warm.

Capshaw tipped his hat and followed her mother to the train.

David turned to Concordia, his frown deepening. "I know your plans are settled, but *must* you travel so far away?"

She suppressed a sigh. It was a long journey, to be sure, but hardly a trip to the African continent. However, she knew that he had a right to be protective, given the events of the spring.

"My departure will free the lieutenant and his chief to continue their investigation, without concern for my welfare," she said.

"Is there really such a risk if you stay?" He stepped closer. "You know I would do everything in my power to keep you safe."

She breathed in the warm scent of his lime-and-bay-rum aftershave. His reassuring, solid presence nearly had her changing her mind.

She shook her head. "I am grateful for that, truly I am. Lieutenant Capshaw considers this our best course, and regretfully I have to agree that he's right. But do not worry – I will be traveling with Miss Hamilton the entire time. You know how capable she is."

"I suppose." When no one was looking in their direction, he took her hand and put his lips to her wrist, just above the glove. Her pulse quickened. "I will miss you," he murmured.

"As will I," she said, after a pause to catch her breath. "By the time I'm back," she added, squaring her shoulders, "the matter will be cleared up. Then our lives can return to normal."

Or as normal as life could be at Hartford Women's College. She smiled. Teaching and sharing quarters with high-spirited college girls made for unpredictable day-to-day living. Even so, she would welcome the start of classes in September, and greeting faces both familiar and new.

David picked up her suitcase and glanced around the crowded platform for a porter. "And how much longer before we marry, Concordia?" A casual-sounding question that was anything but.

Her smile froze on her lips. She surveyed the platform, desperate for distraction – the piercing shriek of a train whistle, a bump from the pressing crowd, a screaming child – anything to evade the question, *When are we getting married?*

Until they had fallen in love, teaching had been her sole delight and purpose. She loved him, but she loved her life at Hartford Women's College. He could not conceive what he was asking her to give up. How could he? Men did not have to stop teaching once they married. However, no college hired a married woman. The thought of abandoning the only life she knew made her breath stifle in her throat, not helped by the acrid smoke belching from the locomotive.

His posture had taken on an expectant stillness as he waited for an answer. The crush of passengers streamed past them.

Finally, she met his earnest gaze. "I-I'm not yet ready. I accepted your proposal because I love you. I want to marry you someday, but not... now." She leaned in closer and softened her voice. "Remember, if you cannot wait, I won't hold you to your promise."

He managed a smile that did not quite reach his eyes, though some of his light-hearted manner returned. "Ah, you won't get away from me that easily, my good miss." He pulled a small box out of his waistcoat pocket. "I have something for you."

She lifted the red-velvet lid. Inside was a heart-shaped brooch pin, delicately worked in gold filigree and seed pearls. "It's beautiful."

He helped her pin it to her collar, his fingers cool as they brushed her throat lightly. He stepped back and dropped his hands as the train whistle blew. "Safe journey, Concordia. I will be waiting."

Chapter 3

Monday, July 11, 1898
New York City

The trip from Hartford to New York City was pleasant enough, although their compartment was quite crowded after the Boston stop. Her mother was unnaturally quiet, spending most of the time gazing out of the fly-specked window. Occasionally she pulled the telegram from her pocket and re-read it with a worried frown.

Concordia found Stella's situation troubling, too. What had happened to Karl? How would it affect his wife and daughters? She refrained from discussing the matter with her mother, however. Speculation at this point would only be upsetting.

Besides, Concordia had other things on her mind. The book sat in her lap, unread, as she considered David, married life, and how to come to terms with giving up the teaching she loved. Her unconventional vocation as a college professor had been a source of strife between her and her mother for a long time. They had only recently mended that rift and come to accept each other's differences. Her mother greatly esteemed David, and was most anxious for them to marry. Once that happened, mother and daughter would not be so very different, after all. Was that another reason why she resisted marriage? Did she fear losing her uniqueness?

The hackney ride from Grand Central Terminal to their hotel was all too brief. Concordia tried to take in what sights she could from the conveyance's tiny round window. It had been ages since she had last visited the city. Everything in New York seemed bigger, grander, taller – from the top hats of the well-dressed businessmen to the spires of St. Patrick's Cathedral and the grand columns of the New York Public Library.

In no time at all they had pulled up to the hotel drive. The bellman helped them alight.

In the lobby, she didn't know what to gaze upon first: the sparkling crystal chandelier that hung from the from the vaulted ceiling, the tall windows swathed in gold silk draperies, the cozy groupings of tufted green velvet chairs, or the tessellated marble floors, polished and gleaming.

"I feel as if we have stepped into the palace of a Rajah," she said.

Her mother nodded. "Without the elephants." She winked.

Concordia smothered a giggle. Her mother's sense of humor did not often show itself, but it was infectious when it did.

The clerk behind the marble-countered front desk looked up at their approach. "Checking in, ladies?" His glance took in the young bellhop behind Concordia, struggling with her heavy case. Her trunk was checked with the baggage master at the station, to be put aboard tomorrow's express train to Chicago.

"I'm sharing a room with Miss Penelope Hamilton," Concordia said.

The clerk's face brightened. "Ah, yes! That lady has already arrived." He turned to her mother. "I was not aware there was a third in the party?"

"I have a separate room. Mrs. Letitia Wells," her mother said, signing the register.

"Ah yes, the last-minute reservation." The clerk plucked keys from the board behind him. "Mrs. Wells, you are in Room 407. Miss Wells, you are in Room 312 with Miss Hamilton. Oh, and would you please give her this? It just came. It would save me a trip later." He passed her both the key and a thick envelope.

Concordia shoved the envelope into a pocket and followed her mother and the bellhop to the elevator.

The bellhop was just about to knock upon 312 when the door was flung open. "Concordia!" Penelope Hamilton cried.

"You've arrived at last. And Letitia – I received your message yesterday. How lovely to see you again. Do come in."

Mrs. Wells turned to the attendant. "Would you take my bag up to my room? I'll be there later." She pulled out a coin and placed it in his already upturned palm. "Thank you." Concordia handed him another coin.

The youth grinned widely. "Have a nice stay, ladies." He tipped his cap and left.

"What a beautiful room," Concordia said, taking in the sight of the polished mahogany mantel and marble hearth, not in use in the summer. A tea table had been set between two chairs and a satin-upholstered settee. She pulled off her gloves and unpinned her hat.

"Your arrival is timely. They just brought up the tea and muffins I ordered," Penelope said. She glanced at Mrs. Wells, hesitating. "We'll go over the itinerary later, Concordia. I don't want to bore your mother with such tedious details."

"Not at all," Mrs. Wells said, perching gracefully upon the settee. "In fact, I wanted to see you expressly to learn more about my daughter's role in your Pinkerton assignment. After the Inner Circle business, I am worried about her getting involved in something dangerous. I knew I could not dissuade her, of course."

Concordia stared, open-mouthed. She tried to remember if her smelling salts were in her purse, although Mother did seem quite calm. After an awkward silence, she cleared her throat. "You *know* Miss Hamilton is a Pinkerton? And you have kept it to yourself all this while?"

Her mother gave her a pitying look. "My dear, you think you can keep these little secrets, but really, it was easy enough to learn. I got it out of Lieutenant Capshaw, back when you and Miss Hamilton were in the hospital last spring. I could not help but wonder at the lady's role in that business."

"I can see where Concordia gets her discernment," Penelope said, grinning. "Let me assure you, there is no need for concern. She will merely be my travel companion, while I am assigned as a train-spotter."

Her mother frowned. "What's a train-spotter?"

Concordia leaned forward in excitement. "I've read about spotters. Railway companies hire them to monitor their employees."

"Indeed," Penelope said. "And most are hired through the Pinkerton Agency. Their purpose is to ensure that conductors aren't skimming fares, and are abiding by the employee conduct manual."

"Train-spotters are typically men, are they not?" Concordia asked.

"The conductors have come to expect and even identify some of the male spotters from our agency," Penelope said. "Women spotters are a recent phenomenon. It has been most effective. We are less likely to arouse suspicion."

"Is there any danger if you are caught?" Mrs. Wells asked.

Penelope smiled. "I am never caught."

Mrs. Wells sipped her tea in skeptical silence.

As Concordia reached for a muffin, the clerk's envelope peeked out of her pocket. "Oh! This is for you." She passed it to Penelope.

The lady pulled out their train tickets and skimmed through the letter with a frown. Then she jumped up abruptly and began to pace, crossing back and forth from the windows to the armoire and back again.

"Bad news?" Mrs. Wells asked.

Penelope stopped pacing. "I regret that I was mistaken in what I just told you."

"What is it?" Concordia asked.

"Our assignments have been changed." Penelope sank into the chair with a sigh.

"Wait a minute," Concordia said. "*Our* assignments? I'm only supposed to be your companion."

"Not any more. You've been given my assignment as train-spotter, and I've been given a new one."

Concordia could not believe her ears. "Assignment as train-spotter," she echoed. "Why?"

"I now have a more urgent assignment. I cannot do both," Penelope said.

"What's your assignment?"

"I regret I cannot say. But train-spotting is simple really, and the Pinkerton Agency trusts that I can train you. I will take on a supervisory role. I'm sure you will catch on quickly."

"Concordia," her mother said, eyes narrowing. She leaned forward and put a protective hand on her arm. "I don't like it. Sneaking around, watching people covertly, and then writing up reports about them? You are taking this trip to escape the danger of the Inner Circle, not to embrace another sort of danger."

Her mother raised a valid point. "Couldn't you bring in another woman from the agency?" Concordia asked Penelope.

"There's no one else at hand. The agency is most insistent that it be you." Penelope sighed. "The price of the railway ticket, as it were."

Mrs. Wells stood, brushing off her skirts. "I'll leave you two to discuss this further while I get settled in my room." She regarded Concordia with troubled eyes. "You'll visit me later? We'll talk."

Concordia nodded and her mother left.

Penelope refilled their teacups. "There is one more thing you should know before you decide. The first conductor we were supposed to keep under surveillance on the train to Chicago is dead. You'll be observing his replacement."

Concordia gripped her cup with a clatter as a sinking feeling of dread settled in her stomach. "What happened to him?" She knew she wasn't going to like the answer.

"He was found on the side of the tracks. A knife in his back."

"Murdered." Concordia shuddered. *Land sakes, what was she getting herself into?* "Did someone know he would be watched by the Pinkertons?" she asked, after a long silence.

"Unlikely," Penelope said. "That information was kept confidential between the railroad officials and the Pinkerton Agency. However, if this conductor was skimming fares as part of a gang of thieves, he may have double-crossed them and they took their revenge. But we must leave it to the police. The Pinkerton Agency was not hired to investigate. Nonetheless, caution is warranted." She hesitated. "I understand if you do not wish to continue."

"But what will you do if I don't come?" Concordia asked.

"I will manage," was the curt reply.

Concordia considered returning to Hartford. In fact, the urge to do so was strong. The trip was certainly not turning out to be what she had anticipated. But how could she do so in good conscience, and leave Penelope to handle everything on her own? Traveling alone was dangerous for a woman.

Besides, Concordia was supposed to leave Hartford and stay out of Capshaw's way. And then there was David. Time apart from him would help her consider her future.

Penelope was watching her intently.

"I'll do it," Concordia said at last, feeling as if she had just stepped into an abyss whose bottom she could not see.

Penelope's shoulders relaxed almost imperceptibly as she consulted her notes. "You'll be observing Conductor John Whitney. He's new to the company, though not without prior experience."

"Why does the railroad company want us to watch him, if they don't know him well enough to suspect him of wrongdoing?"

"The New York-to-Chicago route is a popular run for bunco steerers and other sorts of confidence men. We are to observe how the new man deals with such people, as well as keep an eye on the conductor's own behavior, making sure he's punching the tickets so they cannot be resold, and not running 'discounts' or similar scams."

Concordia raised a skeptical brow. "I know nothing about crooked dealings. How would I recognize such goings-on?"

"Don't worry. We have the rest of the day to go over what you need to know. We'll also review the agency's log-entry system." Penelope crossed over to the desk and picked up a slim volume of black leather. "I have a spare journal." She passed it over, along with a pencil. "Let's get started, shall we?"

It had taken the rest of the afternoon. Concordia felt as if her head was full to bursting with more information than she could properly absorb. How was she to remember it all? Who knew a Pinkerton had so many rules to follow? There was a procedure for everything, from following a suspect to writing a report to taking a person into custody and turning him over to the police – a duty she hoped she would never have to perform.

She then spent the evening with her mother, discussing her decision to continue with the trip. She tried to make the assignment sound as routine as she could, with no mention of the murdered conductor.

"So you see, the task simply entails observing the conductor as he goes about his duties, and then filling out a report. And this way, I will still be able to visit Aunt Stella when I get to San Francisco, and try to persuade her and the girls to return with me."

Her mother frowned. "While I'm concerned for the safety of Estella and my nieces, I do not want to place you in danger in the process. I don't like this Pinkerton business. You are not a detective, dear, nor did the good Lord in heaven intend you to be."

Concordia resisted the urge to roll her eyes. *Can we leave heaven out of this?* "I do not pretend to be a detective, but Penelope needs my help. And if I make any mistakes, she'll be there to catch them."

Her mother sighed. "Some mistakes cannot be mended."

Chapter 4

Tuesday, July 12, 1898
New York City

After checking their luggage with a porter, Concordia waited with Penelope in Grand Central Terminal for the nine a.m. Chicago Limited Express.

She regretted not having the time to take care of any of the shopping errands her friends at Hartford Women's College had requested. Ruby, the house matron who helped Concordia oversee the students in their care, had asked her to buy a stainless-steel sewing needle and thimble set. Miss Jenkins, the school's infirmarian and basketball coach, wanted a fountain pen from Waterman's. Perhaps their Chicago layover would afford her another opportunity.

Although the shopping trip had been denied her, she could content herself with people-watching. It certainly was a lively setting. Numerous sandwich wagons and coffee carts clustered along the thoroughfare, and people availed themselves of these. One fretful boy had been pacified with a piece of stick candy, which he liberally shared with his knickers, hair, and face. A man in an expensive three-piece suit inched further down the bench from the boy and picked up his newspaper once more. Several young ladies, obviously traveling together, tittered behind their gloved hands at the stout, elderly woman with an enormous picnic basket over her arm, leading a pug dog by the leash.

Concordia glanced over at Penelope, engrossed in her book. She was attired in a well-tailored carriage dress of pearl gray, no doubt chosen to better conceal the dust and grime of travel.

Penelope seemed perfectly at her ease, train travel no longer a novelty. Concordia, by contrast, felt like a giddy young girl, ready to jump up and down in excitement. She had not touched her breakfast.

Despite Concordia's persistent wheedling, Penelope adamantly refused to share any details of her own assignment, except to say that most of her work would commence when they arrived in San Francisco.

Concordia had not mentioned her own task in the city. Although she was tempted to discuss her uncle's disappearance with Penelope, she did not yet know enough about what was going on with the Brandt family. Such a discussion would have devolved into pointless speculation. Besides, she wasn't sure her mother would want anyone outside the family to know of Aunt Stella's predicament.

Thunderous vibrations beneath their feet preceded the announcement of their train. People around them gathered paper sacks, bundles, suitcases, and children.

As the train pulled in, the *whoosh* of warm, humid air enveloped her. She hung on to her hat, glancing at her ticket once again. Their sleeper car assignments were in a rail car farther forward.

A smiling, coffee-skinned porter in a white tunic jacket took charge of their cases and helped them up the steps. "Right this-a-way, ladies." He maneuvered with ease around the other porters helping passengers to their seats and stowing away their belongings.

Concordia and Penelope hurried to keep up. "Oh, I beg your pardon," Concordia said, upon colliding with two women dressed all in black, wearing heavy widows' veils.

They murmured something Concordia did not catch, then moved on.

The train was already beginning to lurch away from the station as the porter ushered them to their seats. "Ten o'clock sharp, li'l ladies, I'll be here to make up the beds t'night. Make y'all nice and comfortable." He turned out his palm, face-up.

Concordia had already learned the significance of that particular gesture after a day at the hotel, and fished out a coin. "Thank you—" she glanced at his nametag "—Jonas."

The man grinned widely. "You don' ride trains much, do you, miss?"

Concordia turned to Penelope when he was out of earshot. "What did he mean by that?"

Penelope grunted as she tugged her skirt out of the way of a rambunctious boy running up the aisle. "Passengers tend to refer to every porter, no matter his name, as *George*." She shrugged. "Some consider it simpler, but I find it confusing. I prefer to know exactly who is taking charge of my luggage."

They settled themselves in comfortably, with Concordia taking the aisle seat. It afforded a better view of the conductor, who was even now making his way from the far end of the car, past the rows of passengers. "Tickets? Yes, sir, we are still on time for Pittsburgh, never fear."

She watched closely as the conductor wielded his ticket-punch with practiced ease, dispensed coins in change from a holder at his waist, and checked his pocket watch at certain intervals. Finally, he approached their seats. "Tickets, ladies?"

Penelope handed them over. The conductor punched them and passed them back. "When will the dining car be open?" she asked.

The conductor scratched his forehead. "Soon, miss. They're stowing the supplies we just brought on and are cleaning up from the previous leg of our journey. I just came aboard for my shift, but I understand there was a rowdy group the night before. Conventioneers come to town." He rolled his eyes. "Glad they're off the train. I prefer a quiet ride myself." He made a smooth grab for an overhead bar as the train took a curve. "But the parlor car is open now, if you'd like to stretch your legs a bit. Comfortable chairs, card tables, and bigger windows. Not that the view is worth much right now, the scenery being smokestacks and such-like. Later, when we get into farm country, it'll be pretty. And there's books and magazines you can borrow."

"That sounds quite nice. Thank you," Concordia said.

The conductor tipped his cap and continued down the compartment. "Ticket, sir?"

Once he was out of earshot, Concordia leaned toward Penelope and whispered, "He seems the friendly type. Quite knowledgeable. I didn't see anything out of order."

"Neither did I," Penelope whispered back. "Why don't you head to the parlor car and start on a report of your initial observations?"

"Aren't you coming?" Concordia asked.

Penelope pulled out her knitting with a smile. "It's too early for the card sharps. I'll wait. Then we'll see how our conductor deals with that crew."

Chapter 5

Tuesday, July 12, 1898
En route to Chicago

The parlor car, empty of passengers at the moment, was surprisingly home like, with mirrored sconces on beadboard walls, a small chandelier, a luxurious Turkish rug, and well-upholstered chairs.

Making her way to a window, Concordia grasped the backs of seats as the train bumped over switch-tracks. The conductor was correct – the view was unremarkable. They had left the inner city skyline behind and were traveling through a landscape of factories and coal-burning plants, their stacks belching dark smoke. Although the room was stuffy, she was glad the windows were not open.

"Here, miss, let me turn on the fans," a voice said. The porter named Jonas had entered the car, a dust rag over his arm.

"Thank you," she said.

He nodded and reached for the switch. "We'll open the windows in a little while when we're past all this smoke. Let some breezes in. You want me to bring you something? Cook has the hot water started. Tea, mebbe?"

She smiled. "That would be lovely."

He left. Concordia found a comfortably padded wingback chair beside a rack of magazines and explored the options. She pulled out a month-old issue of *Godey's Lady's Book*.

Soon Jonas returned with a tray. "Lemme jes' set it down here." He pulled over a folding stand. "Is there anything else, miss?"

"No, thank you," Concordia said. She handed him a coin. "You are quite skilled at your work, I must say. Have you been a porter long?"

Jonas gave a snort as he polished the brass lamp fixtures with his rag. "Been doing this goin' on twenty years now."

"I see." This might be an opportunity to learn about the murdered conductor. Even though Penelope said the Pinkerton Agency would not be investigating, it couldn't hurt to learn more. Who knows? She might wrap up that case for them. Wouldn't that be an impressive start to her brief time as a Pinkerton?

Mercy, what was she thinking? Being handed a logbook was going to her head.

She watched as Jonas circulated throughout the room, quietly humming to himself. When he got closer, she took the plunge.

"We heard about the previous conductor who died. You worked with him, is that right? What a shame for his family."

Jonas gave her a startled glance, although she wasn't sure if it was because he had forgotten she was in the room, because a passenger was making conversation with a porter, or because of the subject of her inquiry.

"Yeah, I knew him." He scowled and turned back to his dusting.

"Is it true he was... murdered?" she asked innocently.

The porter shrugged without looking up. "So they say."

"It must have been difficult for that to happen to someone you worked with, every day, over several years," she said. "Were you close?"

Jonas slowly straightened up from the table he was polishing and gave her a scathing look. "White conductors don' mix with the likes of us Georges, and he were one of the worst. I ain't sorry to see him go, no matter how it happened."

She felt a hot flush creeping up her face. "I-I beg your pardon. How terribly presumptuous of me."

The man's expression briefly softened to pity, then to one of polite servility, which she had begun to realize was his stockin-trade. "No matter, miss. I s'pose you don' know no better 'bout such things."

He gathered his cleaning supplies and left her alone with her thoughts.

She wasn't alone for long. Soon the parlor car filled with chattering ladies who swarmed the magazine racks, commandeered tables for cribbage and checkers, or simply found a bright window for their embroidery work. She recognized the widows she had bumped into earlier. They had changed into lighter veils, pulled back from their faces, and shared a magazine in the corner.

The portly woman from the train station took possession of the chair beside her. "This spot isn't taken, I hope?"

Concordia shook her head, wondering where the woman's pug had gotten to.

"My, my!" the lady huffed, vigorously waving her fan at her neck. "These trains get so hot, don't they?" She gestured toward Conductor Whitney, who had just entered. "Sir! Can we get some windows open? I'm smothering in here."

The conductor smiled and gave a little bow. "My apologies, ma'am. I'll see to it." Leaning through the car door from whence he came, he gestured frantically to someone on the other side. "George! Quickly. This should have been done already."

Jonas bustled in, bowing and murmuring apologies, and reached over the seats to tug at the windows, collecting a fair number of coins from the ladies in the process. Concordia smiled to herself. Nicely done.

"Ah! That's somewhat better," the lady said, dabbing her sweaty neck with a kerchief.

"There's a good breeze here. Would you care to switch seats?" Concordia asked, getting up from her position closer to the window.

The lady smiled. "Why, that is most kind of you, Miss–?"

"–Wells," Concordia said. She extended a gloved hand.

"I'm Mrs. Finch," the woman said. "Pleased to make your acquaintance, dearie. I'm on my way to Chicago to visit my daughter and her brand-new baby! Little else would get me to ride one of these iron monsters." She shuddered and pointed out the window. They were about to cross a small river. "Oh, my dear – *the trestle-bridges!* My hands get clammy just thinking of them. How can they possibly bear the weight? It's a wonder we don't go hurtling off the tracks into oblivion." She turned away from the window and fanned herself some more. "I cannot even look. Let me know when we're over it."

After a few minutes, Concordia craned her neck toward the window. "You can look now," she said soothingly, picking up her magazine again.

"Oh! Thank you, dear," the lady sighed.

The rhythmic motion of the wheels on the rails soon lulled Concordia's companion to sleep, mouth partly open in a gentle snore. Concordia smiled and pulled out her logbook and pencil.

As she dated her entry and wrote down her observations of their conductor thus far – a straightforward list, with no problems or irregularities that she could see – her mind turned back to the murdered conductor the man was replacing. Had he been generally hated, enough for someone to plunge a knife in his back in the middle of the night and dump him off the train? Or was it only Jonas who felt that way? On the other hand, perhaps Penelope's theory was the correct one, and the victim had double-crossed a partner in a fare-skimming scheme?

Best that she concentrate on the assignment in hand, she decided, although there did not seem to be much to observe. She had never realized how boring good behavior could be.

The parlor car door opened again, and Penelope came in at last, followed by several well-dressed gentlemen who brought the lingering scent of tobacco from the smoking car along with them. Most striking among the group was a diminutive, ornately mustachioed man in a paisley waistcoat of rose satin. A heavy gold watch chain dangled from the vest pocket and several rings adorned his fingers.

Concordia left her dozing seat companion and moved to a chair closer to the card tables, watching as the gentleman conferred with a much taller man of considerable bulk, whose face

— smooth as a baby's — was disconcertingly devoid of expression.

Penelope joined her, knitting bag in tow. She pulled out several squares, wrapped in wax paper. "I brought us some cheese sandwiches. Did I miss anything?" She brushed off her seat and settled in.

Concordia shook her head as she unwrapped a sandwich. "Were you expecting something... unusual?"

Penelope gave a brief nod toward the tables. "Perhaps not yet," she murmured. "I recognize the small man. The house detective ran him out of our hotel last night. You remember when I went down to the front desk for a spare comb? Quite a spectacle. From what I overheard, he had been trying to run a faro game in the lounge."

Concordia followed Penelope's glance. Two prosperous-looking gentlemen had drawn up chairs to join the paisley-coated man and his large companion around a table. "What should we do?" she whispered back.

"Do nothing but observe," Penelope said. "But discreetly, if you please. If our conductor is at all competent, he'll be by to check on them."

Chapter 6

Tuesday, July 12, 1898
En route to Chicago

The four men played cards into the late afternoon. By then, Concordia and Penelope were the only two ladies left in the parlor car, the other women having gone back to change for dinner. The men spoke in quiet murmurs, punctuated occasionally by the loud guffaw of the man with the ornate mustache. It had been hours since the conductor had made an appearance, although the porter had stopped by several times to tend to them. He would glance over at the card table, give a little shake of his head, and move on.

Two of the gentlemen at the table had lost substantial sums, which they were frantically trying to win back when the conductor finally entered the parlor car. His eyes narrowed at the sight.

"Here now, what's going on?" he demanded. "This doesn't seem like a friendly game of cards, my good sirs."

The men shifted uncomfortably as the small man in the satin waistcoat, derby tipped at a jaunty angle, gathered up his winnings.

The conductor stalked over to him. "I know a card sharp when I see one," he said sternly, grabbing the man by the lapels. "I won't tolerate any monkey business aboard my train. Where's your stop?"

The man muttered something she could not catch. The conductor pulled out his pocket watch, one hand still grasping the man's jacket. "We don't get in to Chicago until the morning. I want you to return to your compartment and stay there until we reach your stop, you understand? I want no trouble."

"What about our money?" one of the men protested.

The conductor sighed. "Did you see him cheat? Drop a card, or draw from the bottom of the deck? Then I would turn him over to the police, but it may be difficult to get your money back."

The men grumbled and shook their heads. "Maybe one of the ladies saw something?" one asked hopefully. All eyes turned toward them.

"Dear me, no," Penelope said, her voice high in distress. "I had no idea. What a disturbing thought! My companion and I were merely passing the time. We paid little attention to the pursuits of the gentlemen."

"Then I'm sorry, sirs, but there's nothing more I can do." The conductor turned back to the sharper. "Count yourself lucky this time, but I never want to see you on my train again." The small man nodded and quickly made his escape from the car, his large, smooth-faced companion following close behind.

The other ladies had gone and the sleeper compartment was empty by the time they hurried back to freshen up for dinner. Concordia rummaged for extra hairpins in her toiletries case. The open windows in the parlor car had made a wreck of her topknot. As she worked the pins, she asked, "I saw nothing untoward at the card game, but I thought for sure that you had. Why did you pretend you had not?"

Penelope straightened up from buttoning a shoe. "It is not our job to intervene in every little injustice. Those were wealthy men who could absorb the loss, though no doubt it pricks their pride. We, on the other hand, can ill-afford to cultivate the perception that we are overly attentive women. Our success depends upon others underestimating us. They must never once entertain the notion that we could possibly be Pinkerton detectives."

Concordia felt a little thrill along her spine at being so casually referred to as a "Pinkerton detective." *Land sakes*, how had she gone from a literature professor to a private eye? The concept boggled the mind. "So you believe that feigning ignorance protects our true purpose as train-spotters?"

Penelope smiled. "It protects *your* true purpose as a train-spotter, dear. I have a different assignment."

Concordia gritted her teeth. "Which you refuse to give me even a clue about. Why be so circumspect on the train, when you don't begin your assignment until we reach San Francisco?"

"It is always wise to be circumspect. Remember, we are traveling together, so your cover could be compromised by me, were I not equally careful. Besides, who says my assignment doesn't begin *before* San Francisco?"

Concordia paused, mouth open. She had not considered that. She started to ask the obvious question, but Penelope gave a thin smile and shook her head.

"Speaking of your assignment," Penelope said, deftly changing the subject, "I would suggest you include in your report an account of the card game we witnessed, specifically the interval that elapsed before the conductor broke up the game, and his subsequent behavior."

"You believe the conductor pretended to be outraged by the card-cheat?" Concordia asked.

"I do. Why did hours pass without the man passing through the parlor car? Most do at least a cursory check every hour."

"He was deliberately allowing the game to go on," Concordia said.

"Exactly."

Concordia frowned. The conductor had seemed such a nice man. She did not look forward to submitting such a report.

"Ready?" Penelope asked, smoothing her hair.

Concordia gave a sigh. Ready? Well, she was ready for dinner, at least.

Chapter 7

Tuesday, July 12, 1898
En route to Chicago

The dining car contained many familiar faces, along with new ones. The train had just stopped in Pittsburgh an hour before, so there were a number of new passengers seated at the dining car's white linen-clad tables. Several waiters, dressed in crisp white jackets with double rows of brass buttons, attended to the patrons.

A smiling maître d' approached. "Just the two of you?" He glanced around uncertainly. "Would you mind sharing a table? Otherwise, it will be quite a wait."

"I have no objection," Concordia said, glancing at Penelope.

"Nor do I." Penelope nodded.

The waiter left them briefly, conferring with two patrons – a man and a woman – seated at a table near the back of the dining car. He returned with a broader smile and pulled out two menus from the stand. "This way, ladies."

A stocky gentleman of medium height, who smelled faintly of pipe tobacco, stood politely as Concordia and Penelope were seated. He made the introductions. "This is my fiancée, Miss Nellie Walsh, and I am Bill Carter."

"We are pleased to make your acquaintance," Penelope said. "This is Miss Concordia Wells, and I am Miss Penelope Hamilton."

Concordia looked at Miss Walsh with curiosity. She was close to Concordia's own age and dressed in a smartly tailored traveling suit of checked emerald, of a sensible fabric that stood up to the inevitable wrinkles of train travel. In fact, everything about the woman implied a well-seasoned traveler, from her sturdy, worn boots and messenger bag, to the short hair neatly tucked under the feathered hat.

"Your name seems familiar," Concordia said.

The lady gave a curt nod. "Nell Walsh. I write the travel column for the Pittsburgh *Gazette*."

"And she has been the subject of newspaper features herself, such as the summer she traveled with Mr. Barnum's circus troupe, or the time an engineer let her drive the locomotive during the Maine-to-Miami route," Mr. Carter added. He glanced at his companion, his brown eyes warm with admiration. "It caused quite a sensation."

Concordia remembered reading about that. *Lady Reporter Tames Iron Giant*, or some such breathless title. "It sounds like quite the adventure."

Miss Walsh grinned. "I love my work."

"And you say you traveled with a *circus?*" Penelope asked.

"Oh yes. Wonderful material for my column. That summer, I was a fortune-teller, a bare-back horse rider, and an assistant to a knife-thrower and a magician. Crenwick the Magnificent is no Harry Houdini, but he's quite good. I promised I would never reveal his secrets." She gave a wink.

The waiter came over to take their orders and fill their water goblets before hurrying on to the next table.

Penelope leaned forward. "No doubt you have another excursion planned?"

"Yes indeed," Miss Walsh answered. "We're traveling through to San Francisco – Bill's my agent, you know, as well as my husband-to-be, and he's making all of the arrangements. From there I'll begin my trip around the world!" She nearly knocked over her water glass in her excitement.

Concordia raised an eyebrow. "My goodness."

"I'll be sending in articles for the *Gazette*, reporting on every stop," Miss Walsh said. "There are sure to be any number of interesting episodes along the way."

Concordia grinned. *Interesting* often meant *bothersome*, at least before one recounted the tale to others. No doubt the lady reporter could make even dysentery sound like an adventure.

"The paper will be running a contest," Mr. Carter chimed in. "*Where will Nellie Go Next?* Readers will be encouraged to address letters to her, with the most colorful ones published in the *Gazette* every week. Those who correctly guess her next stop will be put in a drawing for a prize."

"Will you be traveling along with her, Mr. Carter?" Concordia asked.

"I wanted to accompany her, believe me," he said, scowling. "But I was outvoted by Nell and her publisher."

Miss Walsh waved a dismissive hand. "You worry too much. I'll have a translator and a guide. It wouldn't be at all notable if you accompanied me." She smiled. "A solitary lady braving parts unknown brings out readers' protective instincts."

"And when will you be getting married?" Penelope asked.

"Sometime after the trip. We haven't settled on a date yet," Miss Walsh said, with a glance at her fiancé. "It will be a wonderful happy ending for my readers."

Concordia waited for her to add more to that. One would hope it was a happy ending for the lady in question, too?

"How about you ladies?" Carter asked. "Where are you headed?"

Concordia's pulse quickened. She may not be traveling around the world, or have a fiancé who supported such an endeavor, but she considered her own journey an adventure in its own right.

Penelope answered for them. "We, too, are heading for San Francisco, to visit friends."

Concordia said nothing, not daring to embellish the story.

They were interrupted by the arrival of the dinner tray. Concordia's mouth watered as the scents of braised beef and chicken sauté à la Marengo wafted from the plates. "The buffet on the *Overland* is even better," Carter said, passing the bread plate.

The table was quiet for a while, with only the sounds of clinking flatware against china plates and the hum of nearby conversations. Concordia noticed that Miss Walsh did not eat much. The woman seemed to draw upon a boundless source of nervous energy. She soon pushed aside her plate and wedged herself into the corner of the seat beside the window, watching the other patrons intently. "Uh, oh," she muttered.

"What?" Carter asked, turning his head in that direction.

Concordia and Penelope followed suit. Concordia recognized the small man with the handlebar mustache. He reminded her of a preening songbird, hopping about with his colorful chest puffed out, though this time it was an ornately embroidered waistcoat of Prussian blue with a matching bow tie. Apparently, he had disregarded the conductor's order to stay in his compartment. The tall, burly man with the expressionless face also got up from the table.

"Don't everyone turn around at once, if you please," hissed Miss Walsh, hiding behind the dessert menu. "I don't want him to notice me."

"Is that who I think it is?" Carter murmured, frowning. "Roaring Ronald?"

Now that the man was exiting the dining car and his back was turned, Concordia craned her neck for a better look. "Roaring Ronald? Who's that?"

Miss Walsh gave the man's retreating back one last glance. "A card-sharp and all-around bad one."

"What about the large man with him?" Concordia asked. "He looks far more intimidating."

"That's Myron Krebs, Ronald's right-hand man," Miss Walsh said. "But don't let Ronald's size fool you. He may not look very imposing, but he is quick with a knife. He'll cut you where you stand if you cross him. Even a lady." She pushed up her sleeve to reveal a four-inch scar along her inner forearm.

"Heavens," Concordia said.

Penelope leaned forward, eyes gleaming with interest. "When did you have the chance to 'cross' the man, and how did you manage to walk away with only a scar? This sounds like a story worth hearing."

Miss Walsh gave a weak smile and glanced at her companion, who shrugged. "You may as well tell them," Carter said. "The story's due out the week after you sail."

The lady reporter gave Concordia and Penelope a long look. "You agree not to tell anyone before the story is published?"

They nodded.

Miss Walsh gathered her jacket and handed her valise to Carter. "All right, then. Let's go where we can be more comfortable. I've reserved private quarters." She gestured to the porter. "George, send a pot of coffee to my compartment, will you?"

Chapter 8

Tuesday, July 12, 1898
En route to Chicago

As they entered the compartment, Miss Walsh kicked off her boots. "Sorry," she said. "I'm not exactly a demure miss anymore, and I'm dog-tired. Please, be comfortable." She gestured to the plush, upholstered settees built into both walls. The room was cramped but definitely private.

Once they had settled in and a porter had brought in the coffee cart and closed the door behind him, she began her story.

"His actual name is Ronald Diehle. He runs a crime syndicate in Chicago's western end. Any kind of racket you can imagine – insurance fraud, fare skimming, ticket scalping, bunco steering – he has a hand in it. And he's the best card-sharp I've ever known. Few can spot the sleight-of-hand when he deals a bad set of cards. It's a bit unnerving to see him here." She shivered. "I hope he's getting off in Chicago. I don't want to hide in my compartment all the way to San Francisco."

"Why is he called Roaring Ronald?" Penelope asked.

Mr. Carter leaned forward. "Because when he wins a hand, his laughter sounds like roaring. Such a large sound coming from a small man was noteworthy enough to give him the name."

Concordia nodded. His amusement during the game in the parlor car was certainly voluble. "When did you first meet him?"

"I'd say about a year ago it happened... right, Bill?"

Carter nodded, his forehead creased in worry.

"I was aboard one of the Michigan Central trains," Nell went on. "Roaring Ronald was aboard then, too, and had a game going. It isn't generally known, but my father, God rest his soul, was a sharper back in the day. He taught all us kids how to spot them. When I happened to be in the parlor car and saw Ronald operating on his marks, it was pretty clear what was up."

"What did you do?" Penelope asked.

"I didn't do anything immediately," Miss Walsh said. "Frankly, it caught me by surprise. Usually the conductor keeps a close eye on these 'friendly' games. So I had to wonder if the conductor was either incompetent or in on the action."

Concordia and Penelope exchanged a glance.

"Either way," she continued, tucking her feet under her, "I knew I couldn't expect much help from the conductor. I decided it was time to learn more about Roaring Ronald, and exact a little frontier justice."

Carter gave a disapproving frown. "I have said it before, Nellie. You should not have intervened. Especially without a word to me about it! I could have protected you. You might have been killed."

A flash of annoyance crossed her face before she reached over and patted his hand. "I know, I know. I can get carried away sometimes. Let's not go into that again."

There was an awkward silence.

"It wasn't hard to learn more about Ronald," Miss Walsh finally went on. He's notorious in certain circles. As I said, he gets his money from plenty of shady sources, but he's particularly fond of running card games along the rail lines from Chicago to Milwaukee and St. Paul. I talked to my sources and found a pattern of occasions when certain conductors were working. I decided I'd do a story about it."

Miss Walsh hesitated, grimacing. "But then I got reckless. It made me so angry that Roaring Ronald was getting everything his own way, fleecing vulnerable people – they weren't all rich men who could afford the losses, some were just regular working men who were suckered in. And without even the conductors to look out for them? Anyway, I wanted to hurt him right in the wallet. I talked to a friend I know, who still runs the game. An old pal of my father's." Her face softened. "Not what you'd call an upstanding citizen, but he doesn't prey on those who can't afford it. He agreed to set up Ronald at his own game, match him trick for trick. I wanted to watch unobtrusively. My friend begged me not to."

She rubbed absentmindedly at her arm, lost in thought.

Penelope turned to Mr. Carter. "What happened then?"

He glanced at Nell, who gave a brief nod for him to take over the story. "Diehle didn't take kindly to getting cleaned out. He went after Nell's friend with his knife, and Nell tried to step in. That's how she was injured and... her friend was killed." He handed a kerchief to Nell, who dabbed at her eyes.

"How horrible," Concordia said.

"He went underground for a while after that," Miss Walsh said, blowing her nose fiercely and recovering her composure. "The police couldn't find him. At least, that's what they said. I told them everything I learned. That should have been enough, but nothing happened." She gave a hollow laugh. "Nothing, that is, except for a number of anonymous death threats against me. I know he was behind them. I've written up the story to be published, syndicated in several major newspapers simultaneously. But not until after the steamer sails for Hong Kong."

"What an extraordinary tale," Concordia said.

Carter shifted uneasily. "You will keep our secret, won't you? Nellie's life depends upon it. I would do anything to protect her." His brown eyes softened.

"Of course," Penelope said. She checked her watch and turned to Concordia. "Jonas must be turning down our beds by now. We should go."

Concordia reached a hand out to the lady reporter, who clasped it warmly. "Thank you for sharing your story with us. Good night."

Miss Walsh smiled. "Come visit me anytime."

A harassed Jonas bustled down the corridor to meet them. "I been lookin' for you ladies." He made a great show of checking his watch. "It's after ten," he added, just to make sure they got the point.

"We were visiting a friend," Penelope said.

"Well, I have the gen'lmen's beds to turn down next," Jonas said briskly. "But I didn' want to leave you, in case you needed something from your trunks in the baggage hold."

"No, we're fine for tonight," Penelope said, with a glance at Concordia, who nodded. "Thank you, all the same."

"Well now, you two are the easiest ladies I ever dealt with!" the man exclaimed, grinning broadly. He waved toward the bunks at the end of the car. "I already latched the seats together, pulled down the top bunk, laid out pillows and comforters and drew the curtains a bit. I know you ladies like to feel nice and snug. There's extra bedding under the bottom bunk, if you like, though it's plenty warm this time o' year."

He opened his palm, and Penelope slipped a coin in it. "Thank you, miss. Good night."

Concordia and Penelope decided to forgo the long line to the ladies' dressing room and change into their nightdresses behind the curtains of their beds. First was the challenge of stepping over toilette cases, jars of cold cream, and numerous females huddled in the aisle, chatting and brushing their hair. Grown women, behaving more like hoydens than her students at Willow Cottage. Concordia snorted. Imagine that.

Next came the strange contortions necessary to undress in such tight quarters – she managed to bang her elbow twice along the tiny top bunk – then an exchange of goodnights. She left her light on so she could finish her report.

Although she was honor-bound to leave out the information supplied by Nellie Walsh, her mind whirled with the details of her story. It was too similar to Conductor Whitney's behavior today, and pointed to an arrangement with Roaring Ronald. But she could not specifically identify the sharper in her report to the Pinkerton Agency without giving Miss Walsh away. She had to be content with simply pointing out the conductor's lapse.

Concordia hoped the lady reporter could evade Roaring Ronald until she sailed for Hong Kong. But what of the future? She saw uncomfortable parallels between Miss Walsh's situation

How rude. Who was he, anyway? He carried a satchel and a jacket over his arm, as if he had just stepped aboard. Why would the rail line take on a single passenger in the middle of the night?

Just then, the conductor re-entered the hall. Thankfully, he didn't notice Concordia in the shadow of the platform. "Mr. Tabor, I'm afraid there's no compartment available for tonight, but you are welcome to sleep in a reclining chair in the parlor car. Then we can book your ticket for sleeper accommodations to San Francisco."

Tabor mumbled something Concordia couldn't hear. They passed through the far door and out of sight.

She gratefully made her escape back to bed.

Chapter 10

Wednesday, July 13, 1898
Chicago

Concordia awoke to the early-dawn sun shining upon her face through a gap in the curtains. In the bunk below she heard Penelope stirring.

"Did you sleep well?" Penelope inquired when Concordia climbed down.

Concordia grimaced. "Not exactly." In a whispered voice, she described what she had seen during her nighttime excursion. She left out the part about the late-night passenger nearly falling into her lap. It did not seem quite Pinkerton-like.

Penelope tapped her chin. "That confirms our suspicions about the conductor. Diehle paid Whitney to look the other way whenever a game was going on."

Concordia recalled the conductor's slow, hesitant hand reaching for the pouch the card sharp pressed upon him. "I'm convinced our conductor is a reluctant participant in the scheme. I wish there was some way we could help extricate him from this mess."

Penelope's eyes narrowed. "The man has become entangled with dangerous people – do not forget, there has already been a murder. We cannot safely or prudently intervene. We are to observe and report. It is the job of others to clean up the mess."

Concordia sighed. She had not imagined how difficult it was to be a detached observer. "How long before we arrive in Chicago?"

Penelope checked her watch. "About three hours."

"We have a layover there until this evening, do we not?"

"I believe so."

"Good. A perfect time to take care of my shopping. I should be able to find both Ruby's needle-and-thimble set and Miss Jenkins's fountain pen at Marshall Fields."

Penelope stifled a yawn. "Do you mind going without me? I do not care much for shopping, and I have some things to take care of."

Concordia was curious about what those things might be, but knew it would be pointless to ask. "I'll see if Miss Walsh will accompany me. I imagine she would like a change of scene. Drat, I just remembered. The money from Miss Jenkins and Ruby is in my trunk in the baggage compartment."

"You'd better ask the porter to let you in there soon, before we approach the station," Penelope advised. "It will be pandemonium then."

"You're right. As soon as I get dressed." Concordia gathered up her toilette bag, change of clothes, and headed for the ladies' dressing room.

The train was nearly to Chicago before Concordia found Jonas.

"Could you unlock the baggage compartment and show me where my trunk is?" she begged. "Then you can leave me and return to your duties. I'll be quick, I promise." She pulled the trunk key from her pocket.

The porter gave her a skeptical look. "Beggin' yo pardon, miss, but it hasn't been my experience that ladies are gen'rally *quick*. I still have a lot of beds to stow away, and Mr. Whitney says no one is to go in there. The special-delivery mail packages have to be unloaded first, when we get to the station."

She looked at him with pleading eyes.

Jonas hesitated. "Oh, all right," he grumbled. "But I ain't letting you loose in there. I'm going in with you."

She followed him through two cars before reaching the locked door of the baggage compartment. The porter pulled a ring of keys from his belt, unlocked the door, and switched on the electric light.

"Your trunk and Miss Hamilton's should be over there, miss." Jonas pointed to a stack of cases in the far corner.

Her black-and-nickel-plated trunk had a few more scuffs than she remembered, but was otherwise none the worse for wear. She unlocked it and located the money she needed, tucking it in her pocket. As she locked up her trunk once again, however, she noticed the stout padlock of Penelope's substantially larger trunk had been smashed and dropped to the floor. *Oh no.*

She lifted the lid of Penelope's trunk to check the contents. It was all a jumble, as if everything had been removed and then haphazardly tossed back in.

"What's happened?" Jonas asked.

Concordia stood and dusted off her palms. "Someone has tampered with Miss Hamilton's trunk. I cannot tell if anything's missing. She'll have to check it herself to know for sure."

The porter glanced around the compartment. "Hey! Here's another one." He pointed to another large steamer trunk. The broken hasp hung crookedly, and a dress hem stuck out from under the lid.

"I better fetch the conductor," Jonas said. "We have a thief aboard."

Concordia, who had stooped down to tuck the hem back into the trunk, sucked in a sharp breath.

Behind the trunk was... a hand. "Jonas!" she cried, pointing.

A well-dressed, thin-lipped elderly man lay on his side, eyes closed. Concordia touched his wrist gingerly. It was stiff to the touch. There was no pulse.

Jonas gulped. "Oh, Lordy. Is he... is he... dead?"

Concordia nodded, taking a slow, steadying breath. "I'm afraid we have worse than a thief to deal with."

Chapter 11

Wednesday, July 13, 1898
Chicago

"Here, drink this, it will help," Penelope said, pushing a cup of steaming tea into Concordia's hands.

Before running for the conductor, Jonas had put Concordia in the empty dining compartment, fetched Miss Hamilton, and produced a pot of strong tea, bless him. Concordia held the cup in both hands to keep it from spilling.

"I was calm at the time, but now I cannot stop... shivering," she said apologetically.

Penelope draped her shawl over Concordia's shoulders. "I couldn't get inside the baggage car to see for myself. The conductor was quite adamant. Tell me – was there a weapon or any sign of a wound?"

Concordia shook her head. "Nothing of the kind."

"Perhaps the gentleman had some sort of fit?"

"Maybe. He looked to be quite elderly, and what I saw of his complexion gave the impression of recent illness."

Penelope pursed her lips. "Does anyone know who he is?"

"Jonas swears he's never seen him before. I imagine Conductor Whitney will recognize him. However, if the man died of natural causes, what was he doing in a locked baggage compartment? Could it be connected to the murder of the first conductor?"

Penelope raised a skeptical brow. "Unlikely. In that instance, the man was thrown off the train with a knife in his back. Why leave this one in the baggage car, to be discovered sooner?"

"Perhaps the killer was interrupted," Concordia said. "And remember, your trunk and that of another were broken open. Both are exceptionally large. Maybe the murderer planned to hide his victim after all, but ran out of time?"

Penelope tapped her chin thoughtfully. "That's quite possible. I suppose we will have to wait for the police officials before we learn more. They will have questions for you, naturally."

Concordia shivered again. *I don't want to get a telegram about you stumbling upon a body,* Lieutenant Capshaw had said. Well, he would never hear about it from her.

The news spread quickly. As the train slowed in its approach to Chicago's Union Depot, curious passengers stuck their heads out of every available window. The train stopped briefly so that three policemen could board, then the engineer drove to the switch-track. They were going to be a while.

Concordia's report, sealed in an envelope and addressed to the Pinkerton Agency, was sitting inside Penelope's capacious knitting bag.

"I will report this latest event to the agency and turn in your logs. I have something to take care of while I'm at the office, anyway," Penelope said.

"You don't need me to go with you?" Concordia asked, relieved.

"Not at all. Once we're finished here, you go on with your shopping, and try to forget about things for a while."

Although Concordia knew she would be one of the first questioned by the police, the minutes dragged on. Finally, there was a knock on the door.

"Come in!"

A clean-shaven man barely older than Concordia entered. He was accompanied by another young policeman, carrying a notepad and pencil.

"Which one of you is Miss Wells?" he asked.

Concordia gave a reluctant nod.

The policeman tipped his hat politely. "I'm Lieutenant Freider, miss." He peered at her closely, his brow creased in concern. "You look a bit pale. Can I have more tea brought in?"

Penelope spoke up. "That would be quite kind, Lieutenant."

Freider gestured to the other man, who went in search of a porter.

"Is it usual to send someone so... young... to investigate such a serious incident?" Concordia asked tactfully.

Freider flushed. "I am here to gather information for my captain, who has charge of the case but has been detained." He took a seat across from Concordia. "We'll be interviewing all of the passengers, naturally, but I want your statement first."

Penelope leaned forward. "Have you seen the body yet?"

The lieutenant gave her a startled glance, no doubt thinking her quite ghoulish. "We have a man taking care of that. Miss Wells, why don't you tell me about the events of this morning."

She recounted entering the baggage car with the porter, discovering the broken trunks, and then the body.

"I see. And did you recognize the, er, deceased gentleman?"

"Regretfully no. Tell me, does the conductor know who he is?"

Freider hesitated, but finally shook his head.

"Has anyone reported a family member missing on the train?" Penelope chimed in.

"We're still collecting that information," Freider said.

"Something troubled me," Concordia said. She hesitated, not quite knowing how to phrase the question.

"Yes, miss?" he prompted.

"When I checked the gentleman for signs of life, I noticed his wrist was quite...stiff."

Freider gave a mighty sigh. "Begging your pardon, miss, but I would rather not discuss it. Your constitution may not be equal to the subject."

Penelope rolled her eyes. "*Rigor mortis* is hardly occasion to swoon, lieutenant." She turned to Concordia. "The body becomes progressively rigid after death. It is significant in determining how long ago the man died. I imagine eight hours ago, based on what you noticed, but I'm sure the police coroner can fix the time more precisely."

Lieutenant Freider silently gaped at Penelope Hamilton. Concordia's eyes watered in the effort of suppressing a laugh.

Freider was saved a reply by the reappearance of the other policeman. "The porter's fetching the tea now, sir. Could I speak with you?"

The lieutenant closed his mouth and gave a little bow. "Ex-excuse me, ladies," he stammered, stepping to the door.

The men held a murmured conversation near the open door. Concordia saw the lieutenant's brows lower in a perplexed frown at the words "no wound" and "no weapon."

"All right, then," Freider said, raising his voice, "better transport the body to the morgue. We'll have the coroner check him out, just to be sure, but I see no reason to hold these people."

The second policeman paused with his hand on the door. "Sir, the conductor's asking that the mail and baggage cars be unloaded right away. They are behind schedule. Can I release them?"

The lieutenant waved a dismissive hand and the man scurried off.

Freider turned back to Concordia. "Most likely, we're dealing with a man who died from a fit or some other fatal indisposition. I regret you experienced such a shock, miss. Rest assured, there is no cause for alarm."

"What about the trunks that were broken open?" Penelope asked.

"It's possible the dead man did that. He may have thought they were his, and then used force when his key wouldn't work. The elderly can often get confused."

"How did he get into a locked baggage compartment?" Concordia asked.

Freider shrugged. "A careless porter, I imagine."

Penelope raised a doubtful eyebrow.

"You are the owner of one of the trunks in question, are you not?" he asked. "You'll wish to examine your belongings to see if anything is missing. The railway company will, of course, compensate you for any loss or damages."

Penelope stood, but he held up a hand. "We have some tidying up to do first. It would not do to cause you distress. I'll send the porter to fetch you when we're ready."

Concordia resisted the urge to roll her eyes. Penelope had just given them a lecture on *rigor mortis*, and yet the man insisted on "tidying up."

With a sigh, Penelope settled herself next to Concordia again.

"When will we be free to circulate among the passengers?" Concordia asked.

The lieutenant's lips twitched in a suppressed smirk. She could imagine what he was thinking. *Gossiping females. Cannot wait to tell a sensational story.*

"Soon, miss."

At last, they were free to leave. Those continuing on to points west had another five hours before the train's departure to Council Bluffs, and few were inclined to stay aboard during the interval. After establishing that none of her trunk's contents was missing, Penelope left on her errand to the Pinkerton Agency.

Concordia lingered in Miss Walsh's compartment as the reporter gathered her purse and gloves.

"Thank you for accompanying me," Concordia said.

Miss Walsh smiled. "It's a break for me, after being stuck in here for so long." She gave one last look around at the tidy compartment. "Okay, ready."

"Where's Mr. Carter?"

"Lunching with an old friend," Miss Walsh said.

"Oh, would you prefer to join them?" Concordia asked. "I can run my errands alone."

Miss Walsh gave a throaty chuckle as they made their way to the vestibule. "Bill's a dear man, but he can be a bit... smothering at times. He's become much more protective of me since this–" she gestured toward her scarred forearm, "–and my upcoming trip certainly does not help ease his mind. So we shall have a cozy ladies' shopping excursion without hovering males, and enjoy ourselves."

"Absolutely," Concordia said with a smile. She craned her neck to look for Jonas. With a new crew of porters and conductor coming aboard for the next leg of their journey, she wanted to say goodbye to him before he left. She hoped he had recovered from the shock of the body in the baggage car.

Ah, there he was, in the vestibule at the far end of the car, a suitcase in each hand. "Mind yo' step, ma'am," he warned a particularly rotund woman, who teetered in too-tight shoes.

Once the lady was safely off the train, Concordia approached.

"Jonas, hello! This morning was quite a shock, wasn't it?"

"Lordy, yes!" the porter said, pushing back his cap to mop his forehead. "I'm right sick of dead bodies, begging yo' pardon, miss. It's bad enough to deal wi' getting a couple of coffins off the train, but then having 'nother dead man, jes showing up outta nowhere?"

Concordia frowned. *Coffins?* Of course – the two ladies in widow's weeds.

"Is that allowed?" Miss Walsh asked, making a face.

Jonas nodded. "As long as the bodies are... *embalmed*." His voice dropped to a whisper and he cast an uneasy glance at the two women, no doubt expecting them to swoon.

"Go on," Concordia prompted. "So there were two coffins?"

"Yes'm, tucked behind all them mail bags in the postal section of the baggage car. That's why the conductor was in a dither, wanting to get 'em off the train before the widows got upset by the po'lice being around. 'Course, the express mail had to be handed over on time, too. Mr. Whitney's expected to keep a punctual schedule, no matter what."

Concordia hesitated on the step. The pieces were falling into place. An unidentified body... no wound... no weapon....

She grinned, feeling as if a weight had been lifted. Having a prankster aboard – albeit a ghoulish one – was preferable to that of a murderer. She fished out her pencil and a scrap of paper.

"What is it?" Miss Walsh asked, as Concordia started writing.

Concordia passed the slip to Jonas. "Would you see that this is given to Lieutenant Freider right away? I believe one of your coffins is missing a body."

The porter's lip trembled. "M-missing... a body?" he echoed. He passed the handkerchief over his face again, muttering.

Miss Walsh stifled a laugh behind her gloved hand. "You mean... the body you found on the floor of the baggage compartment belongs *inside* one of those coffins? Then why did everyone believe it was a passenger who had died the night before?"

"I don't know what an embalmed body looks like," Concordia said. "Do you?"

They both shook their heads.

"It may not have been obvious to the police, either. The lieutenant seemed young and inexperienced. I heard the coroner would be examining the body. Has that been done yet?"

Jonas shrugged. "Don' know. I been too busy getting passengers off the train. As soon as the po'lice let everybody go, they in a rush to get right off. Besides, nobody tells me anything 'round here."

"Well, I'm sure it will be obvious to the doctor, but can you see that my note is delivered? Just to be sure."

She could only imagine the awkwardness of the railroad company having to track down the families and open the coffins. What does one say under such circumstances – *we beg your pardon, but we believe you may be missing a corpse?* She took a deep breath to squelch the laugh that threatened to bubble out. That would be in poor taste.

"It seems so fantastic," Miss Walsh protested.

"Remember, there was neither a wound nor a weapon," Concordia said. "Jonas here had never seen the man before. Did the conductor recognize him?" she asked the porter.

He gave a mighty sigh. "This is gonna look real bad."

Chapter 12

The open air of the city street was a welcome relief after the stuffy train, although the buildings already radiated the growing warmth of the July morning.

"I suggest we visit a local notions shop I know, instead of Marshall Fields," Miss Walsh said, as they emerged from the station. "It's a bit farther to walk, but it won't be as crowded. And their selection is superior. There's a stationer's just a few doors down from there, where you should be able to purchase your friend's fountain pen."

Concordia smiled. "I've never been to Chicago before, so I'm happy to rely on your judgment."

"You make a very obliging companion, Miss Wells," she answered, sidestepping a boy pushing a wobbly handcart. "If you don't mind me imposing on you once again, I'd like to send a quick telegram to my editor. The telegraph office is on the way."

Concordia looked over at the young reporter, whose clasped hands and rigid jaw belied her light-hearted tone. "A telegram about Roaring Ronald, perhaps?"

Miss Walsh gave a weary nod. "I learned from the conductor that Ronald is continuing on to San Francisco, aboard the same *Overland Express* train we will be taking."

"Can you board a later train?" Concordia asked.

"That's what I want to ask my editor. The *Overland* arrives in San Francisco Saturday evening, and my interview with the *Chronicle* is first thing Sunday morning. The next available train –

the *No. 3 Fast Mail* – won't reach San Francisco until Sunday afternoon."

"So you're hoping to reschedule your interview?"

Miss Walsh sighed. "It may not be possible. This upcoming week is chock-full of interviews, luncheons, and speaking engagements before I sail."

"As much as I would miss your company for the remainder of the trip, I hope you can make the change," Concordia said. "It would be tedious to keep to one's room for three and a half days."

Miss Walsh squeezed Concordia's hand. "Bless you for the sentiment. I don't mind the seclusion – both Bill and my editor are always after me to rest – but it's the worry. Who besides Bill could I turn to for help if Ronald discovered me aboard?" She rubbed distractedly at her scarred arm. "The local police were worse than useless last time, and it is all too easy to pay off a conductor or a porter."

Concordia had no answer, as thoughts of the Inner Circle once again came to mind. And David. She touched the brooch at her throat.

Miss Walsh gave a hollow laugh and tucked her arm in Concordia's elbow. "Here I am, casting a gloom upon our excursion. Do not worry about me. I will be fine. Let us talk of other things."

Soon they reached the telegraph office and Concordia waited while Miss Walsh sent off her message. "I'll check back in a couple of hours for a reply," she said to the clerk.

Concordia had a sudden thought. "I'd like to send a telegram as well." She paused at the counter, tapping a pencil to her lips. Finally, she wrote:

HAVING WONDERFUL TIME. NOW VISITING SHOPS
IN CHICAGO. THINKING OF YOU. ~CONCORDIA.

She passed the slip to the clerk, along with the fee. "Could you send this to Mr. David Bradley, care of Hartford Women's College's Chemistry Department?"

"That's Hartford, Connecticut?" the clerk asked, scribbling a notation. "Right away, miss."

Miss Walsh waited for her on the sidewalk. "Well now, on to our shopping, shall we, Miss Wells? After that, I know a little tea room that makes the most divine napoleons, along with more hearty fare."

"That sounds wonderful," Concordia said. "But do call me Concordia."

Miss Walsh smiled widely. "Only if you will call me Nell."

The notions shop was indeed a treasure trove of knick-knacks, sewing supplies, and even fabrics from distant corners of the globe, with a selection to rival the sewing department at Sage Allen back in Hartford. Although not terribly adept with a needle, Concordia found herself fingering the burgundy velvet, smoothing the rose taffeta, and holding the lemon silk up to the light, where it seemed to take on a glow. She even had her choice of stainless steel needle-and-thimble sets for Ruby.

"I would pick this one, miss," the woman clerk offered helpfully. "It's on special this week, and comes with pocket-sized scissors."

Concordia smiled her thanks and added it to her growing pile, which included a spool of lavender-satin ribbon, embroidered with tiny white rosebuds down the length. She did not want to greet her cousins empty-handed. One cannot go wrong with a pretty ribbon for young girls.

Once her purchases were paid for and wrapped, they headed back out to the street.

"Ready for lunch?" Nell asked.

"Absolutely."

The restaurant was doing a brisk business at this hour. As they waited for a table, the delectable smells of fried chops and freshly baked bread made Concordia's stomach rumble. The gleaming parquet floor, gilt-edged mirrors, tables topped with crisp white linens, and a high, cross-beamed ceiling echoed the sounds of clinking china and murmured conversations.

She recognized several people from their train, including Mr. Whitney.

Nell followed her glance. "Ah, our conductor. I told you this place is popular."

Soon they were seated and perusing their menus.

"Oh good, the special of the day is the veal cutlet. Best in town. It comes with a salad and beverage for fifteen cents," Nell said.

Concordia nodded and closed her menu. "Why don't you order for both of us? I want to wash my hands."

Nell inclined her head. "The ladies' toilette room is that way."

Concordia glanced covertly at the conductor as she picked her way among the tables. Something about his presence in the restaurant had attracted her notice, and now she realized what it was – the canvas pouch resting beside him on the bench. It appeared to be the same one Roaring Ronald had given the man last night, but she wanted a closer look.

Yes, it was the same bag, she was sure of it. She averted her gaze and slipped into the powder room.

She returned to the table just as their server brought out the salads. As they ate, they chatted about the vagaries of travel and the attractions of the cities along their route.

"How long will you be staying in San Francisco?" Nell asked.

Concordia thought of her aunt and frowned. "I'm not sure. I'm visiting relatives in town."

"It's certainly beneficial to have locals who can take you to see the sights," Nell said, then grimaced. "Depending upon the relation, of course. I have a cantankerous grandmother who insists upon lecturing me about my choice of vocation. She is convinced I associate with anarchists planning to overthrow the government." She sighed. "Needless to say, I don't visit much anymore."

When the check arrived, Concordia reached for her purse. Nell put up a hand. "No, no. You are my guest. The *Gazette* has given me a generous spending account for this trip."

Concordia smiled. "Thank you." She glanced across the room. Mr. Whitney was examining his check as well. She watched as he unzipped the pouch, pulled out several bills, and handed them to the waiter. The waiter hurried back with the conductor's change. Whitney carefully counted up the bills with a nod and picked up his hat to leave.

So, there *was* money in that pouch, just as she and Penelope had surmised. Concordia glanced at her watch. Three more hours before they were to board. "Are we ready?" she asked Nell, as she kept her eye on Whitney. Where was he headed next?

She made her way out of the dining room as quickly as decorum allowed. Nell hustled to keep up, with a panting, "What's the hurry?"

The conductor headed straight for Halsted Street. "Oh! Sorry," Concordia said. "I'm curious about our former conductor." She discreetly inclined her head in his direction. "Are you in the mood for a little investigating?"

Nell grinned. "Always. But only if you tell me what's going on."

As they set out at a brisk walk to keep the conductor in sight, Concordia described what she had seen the night before, when Ronald gave a pouch to the conductor. "It was long after the card game in the parlor had been allowed to go on, uninterrupted by the conductor. Sound familiar?"

Nell sucked in a breath. "Indeed it does. So we know the pouch contains money. Possibly a great deal of money. It looks as if he's heading for the shops along this stretch. Why should we watch Whitney spend his ill-gotten gains? What more do you hope to learn?"

"I don't know, frankly," Concordia said. "Something doesn't seem right. The conductor never struck me as a spendthrift. His shoes, belt, waistcoat – all plain and durable. Not at all flashy or expensive-looking. If he was paid off, why promptly go on a shopping spree?"

Nell shrugged.

They were catching up to him now. Concordia was happy to slow their pace in the hot sun. Her shirtwaist was clinging to her back already. When Whitney went into a jewelry store, she lingered near the window, dabbing at her damp neck with her handkerchief as she pretended to examine the display. She could see the conductor talking with the shopkeeper, who brought out a tray of rings.

"What is significant about him spending the money?" Nell prompted, watching over Concordia's shoulder.

"I'm not sure. Maybe he's purchasing items for Ronald – things that the card sharp should not be seen buying?"

"Well, he shouldn't bother with Mason's Jewelers," Nell said dryly. "They only sell cheap trinkets. Far better for him to go to Donnelly's, on Dearborn."

For the next hour, Concordia and Nell followed Whitney and watched from a distance as the man bought two rings, a bottle of perfume, stationery, boots, and a derby along the stores on Halsted and Madison Streets.

Nell checked her watch as the conductor came out of yet another shop, his arms laden with bundles. "We should head back to the station. I want to check in at the telegraph office on the way."

Concordia nodded reluctantly. She had learned nothing of value from following the conductor. Perhaps she should have found a way to get closer and eavesdrop upon the man's conversations with the clerks, or have discreetly questioned them after Whitney had stepped out of the shop. All she could see was merchandise being examined, paid for, and change given. Some detective she was turning out to be.

Back at the telegraph office, a message awaited Nell. To Concordia's disappointment, there was no message from David.

"We can forward it on to another station, miss," the clerk said. He passed over a slip of paper. "Write out your itinerary. If we get something, I'll send it along."

Nell, meanwhile, tore open her envelope, scanned its contents, and sighed. "Just as I thought."

"Your schedule cannot be changed?" Concordia asked.

Nell gave a curt nod. "There's no help for it, I suppose." She squared her shoulders. "Just a few more days, and I'll be free."

Chapter 13

"Did you enjoy your shopping?" Penelope politely inquired, as they found their seats aboard the train. The long shadows of dusk darkened the windows. Porters switched on electric lights.

Concordia grimaced. "It was successful in some respects, and dubious in others." She detailed what she had seen of their conductor's spendthrift behavior. "What's your opinion?"

Penelope tapped her chin thoughtfully. "I see two possibilities. One, he is giddy at the prospect of such a large sum falling into his lap all at once, and is spending it on items he has always wanted but could never afford–"

"Why go indiscriminately to stores that are all in a row along the same streets?" Concordia interrupted. "Nell pointed out that some of those establishments weren't the best shops for the goods he was buying. It seemed as if the man wanted to spend the most money in the least amount of time."

"That makes the second possibility more likely. Diehle may have been after a particular item he wanted the conductor to purchase for him, but instructed him to buy many things, in case someone was monitoring his movements."

Concordia pursed her lips. That seemed the more likely answer. But what was it that Roaring Ronald wanted, and why couldn't he be seen buying it?

"Certainly you can send an addendum to your last report on Conductor Whitney, detailing your observations from today. Let the agency decide whether to investigate further," Penelope said, lowering her voice as the compartment began to fill with passengers. "But keep in mind what I said earlier. We cannot explore every rabbit-hole."

Concordia nodded. "You turned in my report? Was it satisfactory?"

"Indeed, they are pleased with your progress. Your next assignment is to monitor the conductor on duty between here and Salt Lake City. Don't worry, that will be your last task. Then you are at your leisure."

Concordia sat back with a sigh. The trip thus far had not been what one would call *leisurely*.

"Miss Wells, Miss Hamilton? Letters for you," a voice said.

"Jonas!" Concordia exclaimed, looking up at the smiling porter. "I didn't expect to see you here. Shouldn't you be off-duty?"

The porter grimaced. "Didn' expect it myself, but the porter s'pposed to work this shift hurt his hand real bad. So, I decided to work my way to San Francisco. Got a cousin lives there."

"Well, it's nice to have you here to take care of us," Concordia said, fishing in her pocketbook for a coin. She gave it to Jonas as he passed over their envelopes.

Penelope's contained a small folded slip of paper that she read quickly.

"What is it?" Concordia asked.

"Nothing." She tucked it into her pocket.

The lady's secrecy was beginning to wear thin, but Concordia did not press her further, especially in the presence of the porter. She turned her attention to her own envelope.

Jonas leaned in and dropped his voice. "A po'liceman gave it to me. I expect it's about that mess this morning... you know."

"Oh!" In her preoccupation with the conductor, she had completely forgotten about the dead man in the baggage compartment. How could she overlook something like that? It was fair to say that one does not stumble over a body every day. "Yes, it's from Lieutenant Freider," she murmured, reading.

Penelope raised an eyebrow and shamelessly peered over Concordia's shoulder.

Dear Miss Wells,

While I appreciate you taking the trouble to share your theory of the dead man's identity, we already have the situation well in hand. The coroner quickly identified that the corpse was embalmed, and we are now taking steps to discreetly notify the family before the coffin is interred.

I would ask that you not indulge in gossip on this matter, as it is a sensitive subject.

Yours,
Lieutenant Freider

The nerve of the man, assuming she would engage in scuttlebutt. Faint-hearted gratitude, indeed.

"I must say, this is a surprise," Penelope said. "So the man had been dead some time. How did you know, Concordia?"

"Quite by accident," she said, fanning herself with the envelope. A cool breeze would be welcome, once the train picked up speed. "On our way off the train this morning, Jonas mentioned that two coffins had been in the storage compartment all this while. Remember the widows in mourning attire? It also explains there being no wound on the body, or weapon nearby. But I do not understand why someone would take the body out of the coffin to begin with. Rather poor taste."

Penelope shrugged. "Perhaps spite toward the dead man, or toward the widow?"

Concordia glanced down the car and motioned to Jonas, who had been working his way along the aisle. The porter came back. "Yes?"

"Have the coffins been located?" Concordia asked.

Jonas's forehead puckered. "Last I heard, one was put on a train for St. Paul and left the station hours ago, afore the po'lice figured it out. Don' know about t'other."

"We don't have any coffins aboard now, do we?" Concordia asked anxiously.

"No, praise be, 'cause someone's gonna catch it for this mess, and it ain't gonna be me," Jonas said.

"I suppose it's a mystery we'll never learn the answer to," Penelope said.

As soon as the aisle was cleared of passengers stowing their belongings, Penelope stood and smoothed her skirts. "If you will excuse me, I must attend to something. I'll be back later."

Concordia knew it had to do with the note Penelope had tucked away, but she suppressed a sigh and pulled out her log-book. "I'll work on that addendum you suggested."

"You should be able to post it when we stop in Omaha in the morning," Penelope said. She picked up her knitting bag and left.

Concordia wrote out the day's events, but her mind was preoccupied with Penelope's errand. Was the lady sleuthing? Or meeting someone? She sighed. Penelope Hamilton, by nature a reticent and cautious woman, had kept secrets from her before, but she found it more irksome this time. Was it because the lady was her only companion on this trip across country? While such a journey was exhilarating in some respects, there was a feeling of vulnerability, too, to be without one's circle of friends and family.

She fingered the pearl brooch at her collar. David was very much a part of that circle now. She could not imagine her life without him. She hoped he answered her telegram soon.

It was getting late, and Jonas came into the compartment, pulling blinds over dark windows and setting up beds. He glanced at Concordia, who was staring out at blackness. "Shall I make up your bed now, miss?"

Concordia stood and pulled out a coin, placing it in his up-turned palm. "Thank you. I'll stretch my legs in the meanwhile."

As she passed through the vestibule of the car to reach the next, she found herself reflexively reaching for bars and hand-holds in rhythm with the swaying of the train. It seemed much easier to get around than it used to.

At this time of night, only three passengers idled in the parlor car. No sign of Penelope. Perhaps she was in the library compartment. Their train from New York to Chicago had been without one, but a library had been added for the remainder of the trip.

On her way to the library car, she passed the door to Nell's private compartment. On impulse, she knocked. Nell opened the door a crack. Her face lit up.

"Concordia! Please, come in."

"I hope I'm not calling upon you too late."

"Not at all." Nell gestured toward the folding table strewn with notebooks, magazine clippings, and fountain pens. "I'm writing an article for *Harper's* about my upcoming trip. I fear the words are not coming easily tonight."

They settled into cushioned armchairs. Nell tucked her feet under her, a habit Concordia considered hoydenish among the young ladies back at the college, but the petite Nell made it seem graceful, with a charming at-home air. She seemed so comfortable that Concordia was tempted to try it herself, but she knew she would look ridiculous.

"So, any leads regarding the Mystery of the Spendthrift Conductor?" Nell asked, a mischievous gleam in her eye.

Concordia grimaced. "No. I'm sorry to have dragged you on a wild goose chase."

"If Roaring Ronald has anything to do with it, I'm always curious. Something's fishy there."

Concordia nodded. "Speaking of Roaring Ronald, how will you manage to avoid him over the next three days?"

"Ah. I have an ally." Nell grinned. "God bless that porter. How fortunate it's the same George as the previous leg of our trip."

"Jonas. His name is Jonas," Concordia said.

Nell waved a dismissive hand. "Whatever. Everyone calls them 'George.' They're used to it."

That wasn't the point, but she sensed it was useless to argue.

"He's a sharp one," Nell went on, "and always eager for extra coins. I have enlisted him to keep me informed of Ronald's movements, and help me steer clear of him. Ronald has a private compartment, too, which is fortunately at the other end of the train."

"Did you tell Jonas why you're avoiding the man?"

Nell shook her head. "I made up a story of an old family grudge. George – I mean, Jonas–" she winked at Concordia, "knows Ronald's a shady character, so there's no love lost there. I think the porter enjoys being in on a conspiracy."

"I'm glad you have some help," Concordia said.

"Even so, I'll be spending a great deal of time pent up in here," Nell said ruefully. "You'll visit, I hope?"

"Of course! What about Mr. Carter?"

"He will stop by to check on me, certainly, but it would not do for an unmarried lady to keep company alone with a man in her compartment, betrothed or not."

There was a knock on the door. Both women hesitated.

"It could be the porter. Do you want me to get it?" Concordia asked.

"If you would." Nell glanced at the door nervously.

Concordia opened the door a crack.

It was Penelope. "I thought you might be here."

"Come in!" Nell called.

"I apologize for the intrusion, although I see you have not retired." Penelope's sardonic eye took in the sight of Nell's messy desk.

Nell laughed. "How right you are. What have you been doing with yourself?"

Penelope shifted in her seat and cast a glance at Concordia. "An old acquaintance of mine has just come aboard. I will introduce you both to him tomorrow. His name is Algernon Tabor."

Concordia sat up straighter. "Tabor? I remember the conductor greeting a Mr. Tabor." She frowned. "But that was last night, before we reached Chicago. You say he has just come aboard?"

"So it appears." Penelope gave her a curious glance. "Are you sure?"

night before we reached Chicago," she added, noting his blank stare.

Penelope gave her a sharp glance, and Concordia felt a flush creep into her cheeks. *Drat*, she was babbling, and had undoubtedly brought up the subject too soon. Well, there was no help for it now.

Tabor raised a perplexed brow. "Before Chicago?" he echoed.

"I happened to be awake, and taking some night air," Concordia said, omitting the fact that she was ill clad in a dressing gown at the time. "When I opened the door, you must have been leaning upon it, because you stumbled. I do apologize again for my clumsiness. I did not realize you were there."

Tabor's forehead cleared, and he gave a laugh. "Think nothing of it, Miss Wells. I had already forgotten the incident."

Penelope glared at Tabor. "You told me specifically that you had come aboard in Chicago. Why the deception?"

Tabor pulled at his collar and cleared his throat. "My superiors thought it best that I make a last-minute change in my plans." He dropped his voice and leaned in conspiratorially. "In case my itinerary was known. We believe someone has been attempting to track my movements."

Concordia felt a prickle of apprehension. Please heaven that no one followed him here.

"I would appreciate it if future *last-minute* changes are shared with me," Penelope said frostily.

Concordia tried to smooth the awkward silence that followed. "So you were present for the commotion that ensued yesterday morning, when we pulled into Chicago."

"Naturally," Tabor said, after a pause. He smoothed the pleat of a trouser leg. "However, I've learned not to let such upheavals trouble me. A minor inconvenience."

Although Concordia did not consider the discovery of a dead body and an hour of police questioning a *minor inconvenience*, she decided not to belabor the subject.

Penelope gave Concordia a pointed look.

She took the hint and stood, as did Tabor. "If you both would excuse me, I believe I'll do some reading. A pleasure to meet you, Mr. Tabor."

Penelope gestured to the bookracks that lined the front wall of the library compartment. "From what I've seen, you will find a superior selection."

After making her choice – *Godey's Lady's Book* again, she enjoyed their fiction series – she seated herself close by the viewing platform. Despite Penelope's warning, she fully intended to overhear what she could of their conversation.

Chapter 15

Thursday, July 14, 1898
En route to Denver Junction, Colorado

Concordia had little success in eavesdropping that morning. The rhythmic clatter of wheels on the tracks, the rush of air coming through the open windows, and the chatter of passengers made listening impossible.

She was soon engaged in conversation with a thin-faced woman whose longish teeth unfortunately called to mind a horse. "Where are you headed?" the woman asked.

"San Francisco. And you?"

"We – my husband, our boy, and I – are going to the Great Salt Lake." She leaned forward in excitement. "An extraordinary body of water, I hear. So much salt in it that one cannot sink! Quite salubrious for one's health, too. Have you ever been? No? Oh, my dear, you should go."

Concordia smiled. "Perhaps next time." She glanced toward Penelope and Tabor on the viewing deck.

The woman followed her glance. "My, what a handsome gentleman. A friend of yours?"

Concordia shook her head. "Not exactly. My friend's acquaintance."

"Well, if I was still single," the lady whispered, "I should cultivate a friendship."

Concordia found her eye straying again to Algernon Tabor. A lock of hair had fallen over his brow. He smoothed it back and turned in time to catch her staring at him. His clear green eyes did not miss the flush that crept up her cheeks. He gave an impertinent wink.

Concordia turned back to her seat companion. "Actually, I have someone back home." She fingered the pearl brooch. She had never been able to say that before. The thought brought a different sort of warmth to her face.

The horsey-toothed woman grinned. "Even better. Although there goes my morning's entertainment. I thought I might get to witness the blossoming of an onboard romance. You know – the kind one reads about in the magazines."

Concordia laughed. "No doubt one of the other single ladies will oblige you."

The lady sighed. "It is probably just as well. Reality is no match for fiction, is it?"

"No indeed. Do you read much fiction, Mrs.–?"

"Yarrow," the lady said. "Martha Yarrow. Oh yes, I'm quite fond of books. I used to be a schoolteacher, in fact."

"You were? I'm pleased to make your acquaintance. My name is Miss Concordia Wells. I too am a teacher."

Mrs. Yarrow leaned forward in interest. "Is that a fact? Well, this cross-country travel is making the world smaller by the day. And you are soon to be a missus, you say? Tell me about your young man. What is he like? How did you meet?"

For lack of anything else to occupy her, Concordia found herself telling Mrs. Yarrow about David.

Mrs. Yarrow gave an approving nod. "He sounds like an admirable fellow. When is the big day?"

Concordia frowned. "We…haven't yet decided."

The lady sat back and pursed her lips. "I see. Forgive my presumption, but I assume the delay is on your part rather than his?"

Concordia's eyes widened. "How did you know?"

"Oh, my dear," Mrs. Yarrow said, "how could it not be? Your life will change to a much greater degree than his ever could."

Concordia felt her eyes sting and her nose prickle. She fumbled for a handkerchief and dabbed at her eyes.

Mrs. Yarrow's face softened in sympathy. She patted Concordia's knee with a bony hand. "Now, now, dear. Everything will be all right."

"I - I d-don't want to give up my teaching, but..." her voice trailed off as she blew her nose.

"...but you love him, and want to marry him," Mrs. Yarrow finished. "Of course."

Concordia took a deep breath and calmed herself. "I do beg your pardon, Mrs. Yarrow. I had no intention of crying."

The lady shrugged. "One never does. And yet the world lurches on. So tell me, why must you give up teaching? Just because I and most other women relinquish the occupations of our single lives doesn't mean you must. It's almost the twentieth century, after all."

Concordia gave an unbecoming snort. "No college would hire me once I am married. Can you imagine Mr. Bradley living with me and the female students at Willow Cottage?"

"Do *all* of the female teachers live on campus with their students?" Mrs. Yarrow asked.

Concordia hesitated, thinking of Miss Banning. "No, there are exceptions."

Mrs. Yarrow smiled in triumph. "Then you must be the exception, rather than the rule."

"What about children?" Concordia protested, even as she felt a faint twinge of hope. "And I don't even know if my fiancé would approve of me working outside the home once we're married."

Mrs. Yarrow waved an impatient hand. "There are impediments to every goal. If you want it badly enough, you can find a way." She stood up, smoothing her skirts. "If you'll excuse me, I must locate my family before lunch is served."

Concordia gave a distracted nod, her thoughts already exploring paths she had not considered.

☙❧

Around noon, Concordia awoke to Penelope tapping her gently on the shoulder.

"How about we have lunch? I'm famished. We can go to the parlor car afterward for a round of backgammon, if you'd like." She tucked in loose strands of hair and grimaced. "As soon as I run a comb through my hair. Sitting out on the viewing deck for two hours has left me a bit wind-blown."

"Was your talk with Mr. Tabor successful?" Concordia asked, smothering a yawn.

Penelope frowned. "I'm not sure."

Concordia stood and flexed her back. "I don't even know why I'm so tired. All we do is sit around, eat, read, and take in the view."

Penelope nodded. "You and I are accustomed to a more active lifestyle."

Concordia sighed. "I do miss my bicycle. It seems like ages since I've ridden."

"Once we're in San Francisco, there will be plenty of places where you can rent a bicycle and ride to your heart's content. Golden Gate Park, for instance. In just over forty-eight hours, we'll be there."

Concordia nodded. Little did she know the next forty-eight hours would drive bicycle riding completely from her mind.

Chapter 16

Thursday, July 14, 1898
En route to Denver Junction, Colorado

"If you don't mind, I believe five straight games of backgammon are quite enough for me," Concordia said.

Penelope grinned. "But you won the last two." She began stacking the disks.

Concordia looked over her shoulder as Roaring Ronald strode into the crowded parlor car, accompanied by Myron Krebs. Particularly resplendent today in a bright cerise waistcoat and gray pin-stripe trousers, Ronald surveyed the room and stroked his meticulously waxed mustache thoughtfully.

"This should be interesting," Penelope murmured, resuming her knitting. Concordia pulled out her sketchbook and pencils as Ronald cleared a table and began to shuffle the cards. Krebs gestured with a meaty hand toward three men nearby. "How about a friendly game of cards?" The men glanced at each other, then set aside their papers to take seats around the table.

"Myron," Diehle said, "you mind sitting this one out? It's too cramped for a fifth." His friend complied and took a seat by the window.

Under the guise of their lady-like occupations, Concordia and Penelope watched for the next half hour as Ronald lost hand after hand, doubling his bet each time.

"What's he doing?" Concordia whispered to Penelope.

"Lulling them into complacency," she whispered back. "Watch, he'll double it yet again, then his luck will turn. He'll win quite a sum."

Just as a new hand was dealt, Conductor Gould walked in. His eyes narrowed as he took in the pile of bills on the table.

"What's this?" he demanded. "Gambling is strictly forbidden, gentlemen. Take your money and be on your way, please."

"B-but," Ronald sputtered, face reddening. The other men quickly gathered up their cash.

"Now, now, it's not my doing, sir. Rules of the rail line. Friendly games only – no money is allowed to change hands. Sorry, sir. Just doin' my job." The conductor tipped his cap and moved on.

Concordia bent over her sketchpad, trying very hard not to laugh. Ronald got some of his own medicine this time. She looked forward to telling Nell the story.

"Concordia." Penelope prodded her awake. "Time to get ready for dinner."

Heavens, she'd dozed off. Again. The parlor was empty. "What time is it?"

"Past six."

"I'm so sorry! You should have woken me sooner."

Penelope gestured with her knitting needle toward the large picture window. The pink-tinged sunset sky stretched upon the endless wheat-colored landscape. "I was enjoying the view."

"I only need to put on a fresh blouse and tidy my hair," Concordia said as they entered the empty compartment. The few ladies who shared their sleeper car – many had disembarked in Omaha – were no doubt already at dinner.

"I should not be long, either," Penelope said. "Although I cannot remember where I put my reading glasses. I have the hardest time with the tiny print on the menus." She pulled out her valise and sucked in a sharp breath.

"What is it?" Concordia asked, leaning over.

"My valise – yes, my suitcase, too," she added, opening both "–have been searched."

"How can you tell?" The contents seemed quite orderly, the clothing folded and carefully stacked.

Penelope shook her head. "I have a system for packing. The search was done quite carefully, but I can tell."

"Searched by whom?" Concordia asked. "One of the ladies in our compartment?" She hated the notion, especially since they shared such close quarters, but the thought of the porter or conductor being responsible was equally distasteful. However, they were the only men she could imagine entering the ladies' sleeper car without arousing suspicion.

"I don't know." Penelope's eyes clouded with worry.

"Is there anything missing? What were they after?" Concordia asked.

Penelope gestured to Concordia's own case. "Better check yours."

Concordia rummaged around. "Everything seems fine."

Penelope sighed. "Nothing's missing from mine, thank goodness."

"Should I call for the porter nonetheless?" Concordia asked, reaching for the cord.

Penelope put up a hand. "No, there's no real harm done. I want to handle this quietly."

"It's connected to your assignment, isn't it?" Concordia asked.

Penelope ignored the question. She straightened. "I want to take a few minutes to tidy up. Why don't you go on ahead and secure us a table? I'll be along shortly."

Concordia knew there was no coaxing her to disclose any information. With one last worried glance at Penelope, she tucked her case away and headed for the dining car.

Upon entering the dining compartment, a welcome sight greeted her. Nell, accompanied by Bill Carter, sat at a table at the far end of the car. Nell waved.

"Never mind, I'm with them," Concordia said to the maî-tre'd, as she hurried over.

"This is a surprise!" Concordia looked around and dropped her voice. "Aren't you worried about Ronald?"

Nell smiled. "Jonas told me Ronald is dining in his own compartment this evening, so it seemed safe to come out."

"He's probably still sulking from what happened today," Concordia said with a grin.

Nell leaned forward eagerly. "Oh, do tell. But first, is Penelope joining us?"

Concordia nodded, firmly pushing away her worry for the moment. "She'll be along soon."

"So, what happened to put Roaring Ronald in sulks?" Carter asked, as Concordia slid onto the bench beside Nell.

Concordia told them about the aborted game in the parlor car. "Conductor Gould was firm, but mild-mannered at the same time, even when Ronald grew belligerent. Took the steam right out of him."

Carter raised an approving eyebrow. "The mark of a good conductor. Exude authority, but not aggressively so. Avoid fur-ther provoking an irate passenger. Not easy to do."

"What is not easy to do?"

Penelope stood beside their table, smiling as if she had not a care in the world. Carter jumped up and held a chair for her, but Penelope waved him off. "Shall we proceed to the buffet? It appears they are already out of the sole, but I understand that the lamb is Cook's specialty."

Soon they had filled their plates and returned to the table.

They ate in comfortable silence for a time. Penelope ges-tured toward the open window. "We have been gaining altitude since this afternoon. The air is quite refreshing."

"We have even farther to climb, in fact," Carter said.

"What a shame we're not traveling this stretch by daylight," Concordia said, setting aside her now-empty plate. "It is my first time seeing the Rockies."

"It's beautiful country," Nell said. "If you are up early enough in the morning when we reach Cheyenne, you'll see them in the distance."

"There you are!" a deep masculine voice said. It was Algernon Tabor, beaming down at them.

Penelope started to get up. "Do you wish to speak with me?"

Tabor waved her back into her chair. "No, no, dear lady. It was Miss Wells I hoped to speak to."

"Me?" Concordia repeated in confusion.

Tabor's glance swept over the rest of the group. "But where are my manners? I have intruded upon your dinner party."

"Not at all," Carter said, shifting his seat to make room. "Please join us, Mr.–?"

"Tabor. Algernon Tabor."

"A pleasure to meet you," Carter said, extending a hand. He inclined his head toward Nell. "This is Nell Walsh, my fiancée. She's also the lady columnist from the *Pittsburgh Gazette*." He bent over to retrieve his dropped napkin.

Tabor gave Nell a close, scrutinizing gaze that made the lady flush and drop her eyes. "Ah yes! You write a travel column. I've read it with great pleasure."

Concordia frowned. Was Mr. Tabor one of those handsome, preening men who expected women to swoon in his presence? A pleasing countenance did not mitigate boorish behavior. Mr. Carter had not observed the exchange, which was fortunate, considering how protective he was of Nell. The last thing one would want is a scene in the dining car.

"I was going to propose a game of *Euchre* after dinner," Carter said, "but now that Mr. Tabor has joined us, we could play *Pedro* instead."

"Regrettably I must decline," Tabor said. "I had hoped Miss Wells would accompany me to the parlor car." He politely inclined his head in her direction and tapped upon the leather-bound volume tucked under his arm. "I have a book that I want to share with you. Do you enjoy the poetry of John Keats?"

Concordia glanced at him in surprise. "I'm quite fond of Keats."

"Wonderful! *Endymion* is my favorite. Could I read some to you?"

Concordia smiled. "That would be delightful." She glanced at her table companions as she stood. "Would you excuse me?"

Nell also stood, grimacing. "I have a terrible headache. I'm afraid your card game will have to wait," she said to Carter.

Her fiancé frowned, jumping up and helping her out of her seat. "You do look pale. Can I get you anything, dear?"

Nell shook her head gingerly. "I'll take a powder when I return to my compartment." She turned to her companions. "Good night, everyone."

"The poor girl," Penelope murmured, after Nell had left. "Quite a nuisance to be indisposed while traveling. I believe I will retire, too. I will leave a light on for you, Concordia."

"Thank you. I won't be late."

Several occupants lingered in the parlor car, including Roaring Ronald and his ever-present companion, Myron Krebs, trading sheets from the *Omaha Daily Bee*. Concordia avoided catching their eye as she and Mr. Tabor found comfortable arm chairs in a far corner and settled in.

"May I see the book?" Concordia politely inquired. Tabor passed over the well-worn leather volume.

"Lovely," she murmured, turning it over in her hands. The leather was richly tooled in gilt lettering along the spine, though a good deal of the gold had rubbed off over the years. She opened the fly-leaf.

To John. I'm sure you will be as famous as Mr. Keats someday. With love, Gigi.

Tabor flushed as he reached for the book. "I forgot about the inscription."

"Oh, I beg your pardon," she said, hastily closing the book.

"No matter. Gigi was my sister."

"Was?"

"She died a number of years ago."

Concordia nodded her head in sympathy. "I too lost a sister. But why does Gigi call you 'John'? Your Christian name is 'Algernon,' is it not?"

Tabor gave a rueful laugh. "I was never over-fond of Algernon. John is my middle name."

"And you wanted to be a poet?" she asked. "A noble calling."

"Noble, perhaps, but hardly well-paying," Tabor said with a grimace. "One must accept realities."

"But to go from an aspiring poet to a–" she paused. What was Tabor now? A detective? A policeman? She raised a questioning brow.

A small smile played along Tabor's lips. "I'm afraid I cannot tell you that. My superiors – not to mention the formidable Miss Hamilton – would certainly not approve. I will simply say – with regret – that I am no longer a poet."

"According to Mr. Wordsworth," Concordia said, "a poet is 'a man speaking to men... endowed with more lively sensibility, more enthusiasm and tenderness.' One does not simply leave that behind. Perhaps you will pick up the pen again someday."

His eyes were warm with gratitude. "Perhaps I will, Miss Wells." He began leafing through the pages. "Shall I read aloud from *Endymion*?"

She turned her head to look behind her. The passengers at the far end of the compartment were unlikely to be disturbed by a quiet recitation. "That would be lovely. From the beginning, if you would."

Tabor found the page and cleared his throat to begin.

"A thing of beauty is a joy for ever:
Its loveliness increases; it will never
Pass into nothingness; but still will keep
A bower quiet for us, and a sleep
Full of sweet dreams, and health, and quiet breathing.
Therefore, on every morrow, are we wreathing
A flowery band to bind us to the earth..."

She found herself soothed by Tabor's voice, distinct and easy on the ear. She focused her gaze upon the dark window as Tabor read verse after verse, allowing the words to wash over her.

All suddenly, with joyful cries, there sped
A troop of little children garlanded;

Who gathering round the altar, seemed to pry
Earnestly round as wishing to espy
Some folk of holiday...

As if evoked by the words themselves, she became aware of a child's soft breathing in her ear. She turned to see a tousle-headed boy hanging over her chair back as he listened raptly. Tabor caught sight of the boy and stopped. "Well, young man, who may you be?" he asked mildly.

The boy grinned, revealing two missing front teeth. "What's *espy* mean?" he asked, ignoring the question.

At that moment, Mrs. Yarrow burst in.

"Samuel, you naughty boy," she scolded. "Mama has been looking all over for you." She quickly grasped the child by the arm and tried to lead him away. "Oh! Hello Miss Wells," she added, when Concordia turned around. "I do hope he didn't disturb you." She took in the sight of Tabor and Concordia seated close together with a glint in her eye.

Concordia's cheeks flushed. "Not at all. Mr. Tabor was merely reading some poetry." Surely, Mrs. Yarrow understood that there was no impropriety going on. But why, then, did she feel so guilty?

Mrs. Yarrow met Concordia's eyes with a meaningful nod. "I imagine it helps to pass the time."

Samuel stuck out his lower lip in a pout. "I wanna hear po'try, too, Mama."

"Never you mind, young man. It's after nine! You should have been in bed an hour ago," Mrs. Yarrow said. With one last glance over her shoulder, she led the boy out.

Concordia felt the flush spread down to her neck as she stood, gripping the armrest for balance as the train took a curve. "I must go as well. Thank you for sharing your book, Mr. Tabor."

Tabor stood as well, a hint of a smile on his lips. "Any time, Miss Wells. Good night."

She made her exit with as much dignity as she could man-age, willing the heat in her cheeks and throat to subside. She should not have allowed herself to become so entranced by the man. *Nomadic flirtations*, her mother had said. She would have to be more careful of the propriety of future situations.

The train slowed. They must be approaching Denver Junction. She let out a deep breath. Time to go to work.

Chapter 17

Thursday, July 14, 1898
Denver Junction, Colorado

After weighing how best to observe the conductor in his duties, Concordia decided to position herself in the vestibule at the end of the dining car, out of the way but able to view the controlled chaos of embarking and disembarking passengers through the open door.

The porters, Jonas among them, dealt skillfully with the crowd, helping elderly ladies down the steps from the train, repeating instructions, lugging cases. With one final tip of the cap and an upturned palm, each porter was on to the next passenger. Conductor Gould stood at the steps of the first passenger car, punching the tickets of those coming aboard.

"Here, now!" a familiar voice protested. Concordia stood on tiptoe for a better look. Jonas was arguing with a diminutive lady clad in a richly embroidered dress of red satin, her glossy black hair piled high on her head. The woman murmured something in accented English that Concordia could not hear. A number of other slightly built young women crowded behind. As some of their faces came into the light, it was obvious by the wide cheekbones and the slant of the eyelids that they were Chinese.

"Mr. Gould!" Jonas called, motioning frantically to the conductor.

"What seems to be the problem?" Gould asked, tipping his cap to the ladies.

"We have first cuh-rass tickets," the lady said, gesturing vigorously. "He–" she pointed at Jonas "–want to put us in second cuh-rass car. No good."

The conductor frowned over the tickets she passed to him. "All of you are traveling together, miss?"

The woman nodded. "Finish performance here. Go home."

Jonas muttered something Concordia didn't catch.

"Well, these seem in order to me," Gould said, punching the tickets and handing them back to the lady. "Ten first-class sleeper car accommodations to San Francisco." He turned to Jonas. "Better get them aboard right away. We don't want to run behind schedule."

"Yessir," Jonas grumbled. After waving over several more porters to help with the cases, they got the women and their luggage aboard. Concordia noticed that the Chinese lady completely ignored the porter's upturned palm as she walked past him with a toss of her head.

The train was already in motion by the time Concordia reached her compartment. She stopped short upon entering. Every light was blazing. Cases as well as young ladies cluttered up the aisle, and the chatter of rapid Chinese greeted her ears.

Penelope, hair in a plait over her shoulder and spectacles upon her nose, was in bed, reading placidly in the midst of the chaos. She looked up as Concordia climbed over valises and satchels to reach her.

"Oh! So sor-ry," one petite girl said in accented English. She stopped combing her long, black hair and quickly reached for the suitcase in Concordia's path.

"No matter," Concordia said with a smile, stepping around the case. The girl gave a polite bow and went back to her ablutions.

Penelope patted the side of her bed. "Sit. It's the safest place out of the way." She looked around with a sigh. "It was only a matter of time before our compartment would be crowded again."

Concordia perched on the bed. "Who are these ladies, anyway?" she murmured. "I was outside when they were arguing about their tickets, and one of them said they had just finished a performance."

Penelope nodded. "It's an acrobat troupe, headed back home to San Francisco."

Acrobats? She glanced at the girls. They looked petite and lithe enough for such an occupation, though she certainly was no expert in the matter. She hoped they would not be tumbling in the aisles or hanging from the chandelier.

"They've had a difficult time of it," Penelope added. "Their manager absconded with all of their money and left them stranded."

"How awful. But then, how did they come to have first-class tickets?" Concordia asked.

"A wealthy admirer learned of their predicament. The details are fuzzy after that, as my Cantonese is not what it used to be—"

"Wait – you understand Chinese?" Concordia interrupted incredulously.

Penelope shrugged. "I lived in New York's Chinatown district for a time. One picks up these things."

Concordia smiled. Not everyone.

"So tell me," Penelope went on, a gleam of curiosity in her eye, "about your poetry session with Mr. Tabor."

"Oh. It was fine." Concordia stood and pulled her case from the upper bunk.

"Care to elaborate?"

"No."

"I don't mean to pry," Penelope said. "He's a pleasant enough man, but we know so very little about him. It's wise to be cautious, especially when one's heart is engaged elsewhere."

Concordia ignored the underhanded reference to David, though she felt her cheeks flush once more. "*We* know so very little about him? Don't *you* know about him? You two are working together, after all."

"I do not know as much as I'd like," Penelope retorted. "But I imagine he has orders to be careful with what information he gives away."

"Orders from whom?" Concordia asked innocently.

Penelope didn't answer.

Soon everyone was ready for bed. After exchanging polite nods with the newcomers, Concordia and Penelope settled down for the night.

Chapter 18

Concordia awoke to the pearl-gray dawn filtering through the gaps in her window shade. No one was up yet; all of the bed-compartment curtains were drawn.

Good. She could use the dressing room in relative peace and quiet. She pawed through her jumbled suitcase. It had started out neatly packed, but five days of travel had changed that. It was a challenge to be tidy while living out of a suitcase.

She felt a crackle of paper, and pulled out a folded crossword puzzle from *The Sun*. How did *that* get in here? Penelope had worked on it days ago. Perhaps she had mistakenly crammed it in when they tidied up the other day. Concordia shrugged and stuck it back in the case. With a final shake of her linen periwinkle skirt, she gathered up her clothing and toiletries and slid off the bunk.

Penelope's bed was empty.

She smiled. It seemed she could never rise early enough to get the better of Penelope Hamilton.

Smothering a yawn, she got dressed. Strange dreams had awoken her twice during the night. The first she could definitely attribute to Mr. Tabor's recitation of *Endymion*, as the dream had featured garlanded shepherd folk who danced and sang in a bright, sunny glade. Mr. Tabor was in the dream, too. At first, she could only see him from the back, much like their early encounter when she had opened the door and caused him to stumble. In the dream, she felt compelled to see his face, but when he turned toward her, he had no face. It was just a featureless blur.

She grimaced in the mirror as she pinned her hair. No doubt Penelope's caution of the night before had permeated her dream.

The second dream had been strange, too. She and Penelope had been exploring a dimly lit corridor, but along the way they had to dodge the Chinese acrobats, who flipped and swung and tumbled from one end of the passage to the other. She heard soft brushing noises all around her in the darkness of her dream. Tumblers or rats? Penelope had not seemed bothered by the movement and noise, and plowed determinedly on. In the dream, Penelope seemed to change her garb. Sometimes the lady was clad in her nightgown, her hair down in its customary braid, and at other times she was fully clothed and properly coiffed.

Concordia sighed. Dreams never made sense. No doubt a cup of tea would clear the cobwebs. She was also ravenous. She bundled up her belongings and opened the door of the dressing room.

The foot of a young girl – walking on her hands, Concordia realized in astonishment – nearly kicked her in the face as she stepped out. She and the girl avoided each other just in time, Concordia retreating hastily and the girl springing gracefully upright and sporting a gap-toothed grin.

"Lian!" a voice said sharply, followed by a string of angry words Concordia did not understand.

The girl flushed. "Sor-ry, miss." She ran back to the sharp-tongued lady – her mother, perhaps? – who gave the girl a half-hearted cuff on the ear and hid her smile.

The remainder of their time in the sleeper car would be lively, to say the least. Concordia nodded in their direction, stowed away her belongings, and went in search of Penelope.

Concordia knocked on Nell's door.

"Who is it?"

"Concordia."

Nell opened the door cautiously, glanced down the passageway, and ushered her in. "So nice to see you! Have you eaten yet?" She stopped at the sight of Concordia's worried frown. "Something's wrong."

"Have you seen Penelope? I cannot find her anywhere." A feeling of dread plucked icy fingers along Concordia's spine. *No. She has to be here, somewhere. She has to be.*

"I'm sorry, I haven't seen her since dinner last night," Nell said, brows puckered. "Please, sit. You look terrible."

Concordia sank onto the settee, hands clasped. Nell sat beside her, tucking her feet under in customary fashion.

"I have searched everywhere," Concordia said. "I was hoping she was with you. My next step is to find Mr. Tabor."

A distressed frown crossed Nell's face. "Why *him*? Are they close?"

"Not exactly, but they have been... conversing... from time to time during the trip from Chicago. He may have seen her." She looked intently at Nell. "You don't like him much, do you?"

Nell shrugged. "I only just met him, but I didn't like the way he stared at me last night."

Concordia nodded. "I cannot account for that. Perhaps it was curiosity about a celebrity? But he really is a nice man, once you get to know him."

Nell gave her a look of exasperation. "And how well do you know him?"

Concordia hesitated. Not at all well, if she were honest. But she ignored the question and returned to the more urgent subject. "If Mr. Tabor hasn't seen Penelope, I shall have to notify the conductor."

Nell's eyes grew wide. "That seems rather drastic. Perhaps she decided on a last-minute change of plans and got off in Cheyenne."

Concordia shook her head. "Her belongings are here, and there's no note." She grew quiet, remembering that Penelope's cases had been searched the night before.

"What could have happened to her?" Nell asked. "When passengers go missing from the train, it's usually because they got drunk and fell off. I very much doubt that's the case here."

"She could have been pushed," Concordia said.

Nell's eyes gleamed with interest. "Who would do something like that to a nice lady like Penelope Hamilton?"

Concordia stood. "Never mind. My imagination is running away with me." She had already said too much.

Nell got up and saw her to the door. "If you need help searching, ask Bill. I wish I could help, but-"

Concordia nodded. "I know, you have to stay out of sight. Thanks, Nell."

Mr. Tabor was equally alarmed by the lady's disappearance. "I cannot account for it," he said, a puzzled frown tugging at his brows. "How may I be of assistance?"

"Ask the porter to open up the baggage car so you can search there," Concordia said. She firmly pushed out of her mind the image of the dead body from her last baggage car visit. "I'll check with the only other passenger she knows on board – Mr. Carter."

"Right away," Tabor said, going off in search of the porter.

Concordia caused quite a stir when she finally found Bill Carter in the men-only smoker car. As it turned out, he had not seen Miss Hamilton, either. "I'm sorry, Miss Wells."

She clasped her hands together, struggling to maintain her composure. Her eyes stung with both unshed tears and the smoke of noxious cigars. Where could Penelope Hamilton be? She tried not to picture her friend's body, flung by the side of the tracks.

"Steady, now. We'll find her." Mr. Carter set aside his pipe and stood as several men glared at them. "Let's get out of here and talk to the conductor. I'm sure he'll know what to do."

Chapter 19

Friday, July 15, 1898
En route to Ogden, Utah

Concordia waited anxiously in the conductor's closet-sized office for word. Finally, by mid-morning, the conductor and Mr. Carter – who had volunteered to accompany him on his search of the entire train – returned.

"We've checked every compartment, from the immigrant car to the private suites, and every nook and cranny in between," Gould said, with a shake of his head. "There's not a sign of her."

She struggled to get a full breath. Penelope was *gone*.

The conductor turned to the porter, hovering in the corridor. "A glass of water, quickly."

Once Concordia had recovered her composure, she said, "Miss Hamilton must be somewhere along the... tracks. Can you search for her?"

Conductor Gould pulled out his watch. "We get to Granger in twenty-two minutes. The stationmaster there can telegraph all the stations along the route. When did you first discover her missing?"

She paused. "Shortly after five in the morning."

"That would be after the Cheyenne stop, then. And you say you last saw her when you went to bed, about an hour after we pulled out of Denver Junction? We had to have been past Brighton by then. All right, between Brighton and Cheyenne, let's say."

Concordia rummaged in her pocket for a handkerchief. The conductor passed her a large one of clean cotton. "Try not to worry, miss. We may get word when we stop in Granger that your friend has been found safe."

Concordia looked in his eyes, but saw no hope there. She sat up straighter. "When we stop, I wish to send a telegram as well."

The conductor frowned. "It's a bit soon to be notifying next of kin."

"No, no, it's not that. Nevertheless, it's quite urgent." She had to notify the Pinkerton Agency and figure out what to do. Should she go on, or turn back? Would the agency help in the search?

He sighed. "Very well, but if you don't get an immediate reply, tell the station master to send the message along to Ogden. You can check when we pull in there. We must stay on schedule."

Concordia and Mr. Carter sat with Nell in her compartment. The train had been stopped in Granger for several minutes now, and Concordia waited impatiently for the conductor to escort her to the telegraph office.

Nell and Mr. Carter seemed to understand her need for quiet, and did not try to make conversation. She noticed they exchanged worried glances from time to time when they thought she wasn't looking.

At last, there was a knock on the door. Carter opened it. To Concordia's disappointment, it was Mr. Tabor, not Mr. Gould.

"I have not seen such long faces since the Panic of '93," Tabor quipped, crossing the room in long strides. He nodded to Nell and Carter. "Good morning."

"Not such a good morning," Nell muttered under her breath.

"I thought you were the conductor," Concordia said. "I want to send a telegram from the station."

"I just sent one myself. Mr. Gould asked me to fetch you. Come on, there isn't much time." He offered his arm.

With a nod of goodbye to Nell and Mr. Carter, Concordia hurried with Tabor to the telegraph office.

Concordia had the note already prepared.

MISS H DISAPPEARED. SEARCH COMMENCING. PLS ADVISE NEXT STEP: CONTINUE ON WITH HER TASK? TABOR STILL ABOARD. ~C. WELLS.

Fortunately, the telegraph address Penelope had given her in case of emergency had not a hint of "Pinkerton" in the direction, merely the secretary's name and street address.

She handed the slip to the telegraph operator. "Can you make sure any reply is forwarded on to Ogden?"

The clerk set the slip aside. "Aye, I will."

She fished in her purse for money, but Tabor stopped her. "I've already taken care of it."

"Thank you." She turned to the telegrapher, who was straightening his desk. "I'd like you to send it *now*. It's most urgent."

"I just sent out a passel o' *urgent* messages. I gots things ta do, missy," the man snarled.

"And I have a train to catch," she snapped back. "Why don't you send it now and save us all some time."

After launching a poorly-aimed stream of tobacco juice at the heavily-stained spittoon in the corner, the man sat down and began transmission.

"We really must go," Tabor said, when the man had finished. She gave a resigned nod and let him lead the way.

"Can we talk?" she asked, as Tabor helped her aboard. "Somewhere private," she added.

"Of course."

The parlor and dining cars were much too crowded at this hour, but they had the viewing platform to themselves. "The plains have their own sort of beauty," she said absently, watching as swathes of buffalo grass rippled in the breeze and dotted herds grazed in the distance. Penelope would have enjoyed the view. Concordia felt a dull ache in her chest.

Jonas stepped through the door, his forehead creased in a frown. "Can I get you something, miss? You ain't had a thing to eat all morning, if you don' mind me sayin' so."

"I'm not feeling all that hungry," she said wearily.

"Lemme at least get you some tea," he coaxed.

She nodded. "Thank you."

When the porter had left, she turned to Tabor. "Would you be permitted to stay behind and join the search for Miss Hamilton?"

Tabor grimaced. "As much as I would like to, Miss Wells, I doubt the powers-that-be would permit it. I have telegraphed for instructions, so we shall see. Like you, I expect to receive a reply in Ogden this afternoon. I doubt I would be of much help in a search, however. These railway fellows are more experienced in such matters."

"What if she was pushed off the train?"

Tabor gave her a startled look. Was the notion new to him, or was he shocked by a woman broaching such an indelicate subject?

Jonas emerged with a tea tray. As he set up the folding stand, she noticed he had taken the liberty of adding toast and jam. Bless the man. Perhaps she could eat a little something, after all. She gave him a grateful look.

Tabor fished a coin out of his vest pocket. "That will be all, George."

Jonas's face took on a shuttered expression as he bowed and pocketed the coin.

Tabor crossed his long legs, settling himself for a long talk. "'What if she was pushed?'" he mused, repeating Concordia's question. "That has been worrying me as well. It's possible that someone targeted Miss Hamilton because of her association with me."

She nodded. "I fear that is so. Her belongings were searched yesterday."

Tabor leaned forward in interest. "Yesterday – when? Was anything taken?"

"She said nothing was missing. We don't know exactly when it happened – sometime in the afternoon, before we went to dinner." Concordia lifted a quizzical brow. "Are you not in the same danger? You are working together, after all."

Tabor smiled. "I can take care of myself, do not worry. As for Miss Hamilton... well, she was keeping something from me. She appeared to resent my being brought into this case, and wanted to work it alone."

"Keeping something from you? What?" she asked. She had sensed no resentment on Penelope's part, merely caution toward Algernon Tabor.

Tabor shook his head, a hint of a patronizing smile playing on his lips.

Concordia abruptly stood, quivering with indignation. "Do not play games with me, Mr. Tabor. My best friend and only companion on this journey is most likely... dead, and I have not a shred of patience left."

Tabor's expression turned to one of distress. "Dear lady, please sit," he pleaded. "People are beginning to look."

"Let them."

Tabor sighed. "Very well, I'll tell you more about the matter, but only because you are likely in danger yourself. Now, would you *please* sit down?"

She sat. "How am *I* in danger?"

"By your association with Miss Hamilton and myself, unfortunately." Tabor leaned closer and reached into his jacket pocket. He pulled out a slim leather billfold and opened it up for her to see. She sucked in a breath when she saw the silver star, and *U.S. Secret Service* imprinted above it.

"This is my badge and commission book," he said quietly. "There's my name, see?"

Sure enough, "Algernon G. Tabor" was visible on the card, in faded ink.

"I don't understand," Concordia said. "The Secret Service and the Pinkerton Agency are working together?"

"It's not unheard-of for federal law enforcement to make use of Pinkerton's services. All too often we are stretched thinly. In this instance, the case landed in the lap of the Pinkerton Agency first."

"What are you working on?"

A pained look crossed Tabor's face. "I would rather not go into the particulars, for your own safety. I imagine your agency will not want you embroiled in this any further, either, but we'll know more when we reach Ogden."

"I feel so helpless," she said, dropping her eyes.

"There's one thing you can do," Tabor said. "Are Miss Hamilton's belongings still in your compartment?"

"Yes."

"If it wouldn't offend your sensibilities, would you go through her things? She may have left a journal or log, something to give us a clue about her disappearance, and who is responsible."

She grimaced. It was a terrible violation of privacy, but she saw no other option. "All right. I'll do it."

Chapter 20

Friday, July 15, 1898
En route to Ogden, Utah

The sleeper car was mercifully devoid of tumbling acrobats at the moment. Concordia tugged at the suitcase beneath Penelope's seat and opened it. She fought back the tears that pricked her eyes. Would she ever see her again? The thought was unbearable. She had never felt so alone in her life.

The contents of Penelope's case were neatly arranged, her undergarments separated from her toiletries, her shirtwaists from her skirts, everything folded. Rather extraordinary, Concordia thought, remembering the state of her own case.

Feeling like a snoop, Concordia nonetheless unfolded and shook out every item, groped in the toes of Penelope's shoes, probed the linings and pockets of the case. Nothing. Where could her log be? Concordia knew she kept one. Had it been stolen?

She explored Penelope's knitting bag next, but found nothing unusual until she came upon one particular ball of yarn. The cardboard the yarn was wrapped around was actually two pieces of cardboard, glued together. One end had been pried apart.

Heart beating faster, Concordia reached in and extracted a tiny gray cloth pouch with gold stamping. The pouch itself was empty. She examined the outside of it. Some of the stamping had rubbed off over time, but several numbers and letters were visible. *First Nat* and the numbers *1* and *3*, along with the upper left curve of what could be either an *8* or a *9*.

The bag had held a bank's safe-deposit box key.

But who had it now? Had Penelope removed it from the pouch and kept it on her person after she discovered her belongings were searched? Or had the searcher found it first, and Penelope had not wanted to admit it to Concordia?

She was keeping something from me, Tabor had said. Did he mean information, or this key?

The bigger question: could Concordia trust Tabor? She did not know the answer to that, either, but he was her only remaining link to the case. Finding out more from him could lead her to Penelope. She must be allowed to continue working with him in order to do so.

She prayed that a favorable message awaited her in Ogden.

She shared her discovery with Tabor just before they reached the station in Ogden. The man's eyes narrowed as he turned over the pouch in his hand. "Even without the key, this gives me a location. It must be the First National Bank."

"The First National Bank," she repeated, not commenting upon the "me" in Tabor's statement. "In San Francisco, I presume?"

Tabor nodded. "The corner of Bush and Sansome. I can use this pouch to persuade them to open the box, telling them the key has been lost."

She plucked the bag out of his grasp. "You may have this *after* you answer some questions."

Tabor shifted uneasily upon the bench, but made no move to snatch it back.

"What do you believe is contained in the bank box?" she asked.

In the exasperating silence that followed, Concordia reflected upon what she knew. The Secret Service. What kind of cases did they handle? They were part of the Treasury Department, were they not? And treasury officials would be concerned with money....

Could there be stolen money in the box? No, that made no sense. Why steal money from one bank, only to put it in another?

Chapter 21

Friday, July 15, 1898
En route to San Francisco, California

Concordia kept to her seat for the rest of the afternoon, finishing her report on the conductor. Although the Pinkerton Agency had dismissed her, she wanted to finish her assignment properly. Besides, the conductor deserved a glowing report. Worthy of note was his fair dealing with the Chinese lady acrobats, his kindness to Concordia throughout the ordeal of Penelope's disappearance, and his handling of Roaring Ronald - who had not run a card game since.

There had been no progress in locating Penelope Hamilton. Stations along the line had reported no sign of her. Only a few stations remained to check in. Concordia tried to take comfort in the news that no body had been found, but if Penelope had gotten off the train by her own choice, why had she not sent word?

When she had finished her report and sealed it in an envelope, she gazed idly through the window, watching the scenery go by. She was too distracted for reading and not in the mood for conversation, not even with Nell. As far as Tabor was concerned, she had no more items of Penelope's to leverage in exchange for further information. She found his sense of self-importance and distrust of Penelope's motives vexing. She wished she could wash her hands of him. She did not have that luxury. She would certainly be tagging along when Tabor investigated the bank deposit box, whether he wanted her company or not.

The train had left Ogden and Salt Lake City long ago, and they were traversing the bleak landscape of the Great Desert. After staring at nothing in the dusky light but brown, bare terrain, broken up by occasional clumps of sagebrush, she decided to change into her dinner dress and pull out her journal. Perhaps if she wrote out her thoughts about this tangle, something might become clearer before they reached San Francisco tomorrow evening.

The compartment began to fill with members of the young acrobat troupe, chattering and laughing.

"Excuse, miss?" a soft voice asked. Concordia looked up from the page to see Lian, the young girl she had nearly collided with this morning. The girl held out a small bit of paper, intricately folded in the shape of a dove. "*Zhezhi,* for you."

"How lovely," Concordia said, cradling it in her hands. "Thank you! But why?" She looked over the girl's head at the older woman standing behind her.

"Lian want to make something for you, to say sor-ry about today," the woman explained. She smoothed the girl's hair fondly.

"That's quite all right, really," Concordia said to the girl with a smile. "What is... zhe... zhe..." her voice trailed off.

"*Zhezhi,*" the woman finished. "Chinese paper folding." With a bow, she turned to leave for their seats.

"Wait, I am curious," Concordia said. "Your – daughter? She is so young. Does she really perform with your group?"

The woman's eyes took on a mischievous glint. "You like to see?" She gestured to Lian and another young lady. "Watch."

Concordia watched in amazement as the older girl grasped Lian's wrists, and in one fluid motion, Lian swung atop the girl's shoulders, then moved with ease into a steady handstand. "Amazing," she murmured.

"Ceiling not high enough here," the woman said. "Usually Lian balance pole and plates, too, while on Shu-Lee's shoulders."

It was at this unpropitious moment that Jonas entered the compartment. "Lordy!" he exclaimed, taking in the sight. The startled girl kicked the ceiling's chandelier, which swung alarmingly as she jumped down.

"Ain't gettin' paid near 'nuff to deal wi' crazy girls," the porter muttered under his breath.

Concordia hid a smile, recalling occasions at Hartford Women's College when Ruby, the house matron, would grumble at the high jinks of the students in their charge. None had been tumblers, of course. Ruby did not know what she was missing.

Thoughts of Ruby and the doings at Willow Cottage made her feel homesick again. She had been away less than a week and missed everyone already.

Jonas came over to her seat. "I jes' came to check, now that I have a free moment, miss. Did you get the telegram?"

"Yes, you gave me two in Ogden, remember?" Maybe the stress of acrobats in the aisles was getting to the porter.

Jonas shook his head. "No, there was another one, at Salt Lake. Mr. Tabor offered to give it to you, 'cause I was busy gettin' passengers off the train, an' a lot of the crew was changing shifts."

She sat up straighter. "Another telegram, you say? Who was it from?"

"Dunno, miss." The porter frowned. "I hope you're not mad I gave it t'him. Seein' as how you two been real friendly and spending time together, I thought—" he hesitated.

Her jaw clenched. She did not long wonder what Jonas, or anyone else, thought of her and Tabor. No doubt, Tabor had exaggerated their closeness in order to get the telegram from the porter. Blast the man.

"My apologies miss. I'll go get it from him right away," the porter said, turning to leave.

"Never mind," she said, standing with a scowl. She impatiently twitched her skirts out of the way. "I'll get it."

Jonas gave a small chuckle as she left. "I feel right sorry for Mr. Tabor."

She found Tabor in the rapidly filling dining car, working on a plate of roast beef, string beans *béarnaise*, and new potatoes. She did not recognize any of his dining companions, but all the men at the table stood politely as she approached. She fought to keep her temper in check. It would not do to make a scene in such a place.

"Do you care to join us, Miss–?" one of the gentlemen hesitated.

"–Wells," Concordia said. "No, thank you." She turned to Tabor. "May I speak with you?" She kept her voice even.

Tabor blotted his lips with a napkin, but Concordia did not miss the wary set of his features. "Can it wait, dear lady? I am nearly finished."

She glanced around uneasily. She was blocking the narrow aisle and drawing unwanted attention. Ronald Diehle, sitting alone at his table, gazed at her curiously, as did other patrons. A waiter squeezed past her with a fully laden tray. Best to get this over with.

"Apparently, I have already been waiting – for my telegram," she said icily.

Tabor lifted his face in a puzzled frown of innocence. "Telegram?"

"The one Jonas gave you to give to me. When the train stopped in Salt Lake City."

His frown deepened. "Jonas? Ah yes, the porter. I'm sorry, Miss Wells, but he never gave me a telegram. Why would he do so?" His dark-lashed eyes regarded her in amusement as he raised his voice. "After all, I am not your husband, am I?"

She heard Roaring Ronald chortle. Her face flushed. Tabor was insufferable.

She took a steadying breath. "Whether or not the porter should have given you my telegram is immaterial. When you are finished here, I expect you to restore it to me." She struggled to keep her voice low, but in her agitation, it rose of its own accord. Face flaming, she flounced out of the car, every eye upon her.

the viewing platform door at the far end was open. She did not bother to turn on more lights. Her eyes would only have to re-adjust.

She traversed the car in the gloom, dodging – with varying degrees of success – occasional tables, book racks, wing chairs, and foot stools. She stepped through the door, which was in-deed wide open, and hesitated on the viewing platform. Her neck prickled as she sensed movement.

She was not alone.

Concordia gasped as a half-moon spilled dim light along the deck. A man's form lay sprawled, face down.

Was he drunk, or worse? Her limbs shook, but she took a tentative step toward the form. The strong breeze blew her hair into her eyes. She swiped it away impatiently. The moonlight illuminated the hilt of a knife plunged into the man's back.

Her shriek was swallowed up in the blowing wind and the steady clatter of wheels upon tracks. She collapsed in a dead faint.

Chapter 23

Concordia awoke on a hard surface, blinking up at the pre-dawn sky. She felt chilled and her head ached. Why wasn't she in her own berth?

Then she remembered. She sat up abruptly. The man was still lying face down beside her on the platform, a red lacquer hilt sticking out of his back. Knowing he must be dead, she nonetheless reached a shaking hand under his jacket to feel for a heartbeat. No flutter, no breath. Nothing. Bracing herself, she leaned in closer, tugging at the man's shoulder so she could see his face. She had a feeling she already knew who it was.

Algernon Tabor stared sightlessly back.

She shuddered and stood, brushing off her skirts. She should get help.

Inexplicably, the door was now closed and locked. She pushed and rattled the handle to no avail. The curtains were drawn across the glass. She was sure she had left the door open behind her.

She remembered the sense that someone had been moving nearby when she first stepped out on the platform. It had certainly not been Mr. Tabor. Now that she reflected on it, the sound had come from behind. Had she interrupted the murderer, before he could dispose of the body over the railing? Her stomach clenched at the thought. The killer might have hidden behind one of the large wing chairs when she entered the compartment, waiting to see what would happen.

But why not dispose of her as well?

She hugged her arms over her chest, shivering in the chill of early morning. Why kill Tabor? Was Roaring Ronald to blame? Had there been a falling out between them, or had Tabor changed his mind about risking his career for whatever scheme Ronald had proposed?

She knew what she had to do next, distasteful as it was. Suppressing another shudder, she groped in the dead man's pockets, hoping to find her telegram and the pouch she had relinquished to him. Neither was on his person, although his other personal items – watch, money clip, Secret Service badge – were intact.

She stepped away and turned back to the door. She kept her face to the small gap in the curtains, ready to rap upon the glass as soon as anyone appeared in the library car. It was useless to yell or pound on the door before then. The outside noise was too great.

She sighed. This was no innocuous case of a body without a casket. This man was most definitely murdered, and with him was gone her one link to Penelope.

Chapter 24

Saturday, July 16, 1898
En route to San Francisco, California

It was Jonas, bless him, who finally came through the library car and opened the door in response to Concordia's frantic rapping on the glass. "What the–?" His breath caught in a low whistle between his teeth as he caught sight of the body.

"He's dead," she said miserably.

"I can see that." Jonas said. "Lordy. Why you alw'ys finding dead bodies, miss?" He pointed at the knife in Tabor's back. "That ain't no accident."

"No."

"When was this?" Jonas asked. He gestured to the platform. "And how'd you get locked out?"

She explained her late-night visit to the library, and her sense that someone had moved behind her. "The killer may have been hiding and locked the door while I was insensible." She touched her scalp and winced.

"Are you all right?" Jonas asked.

"I seem to have hit my head when I fainted," she said sheepishly. "I generally have a stronger constitution than that."

"If it was me, findin' him in the dark like that... I'd still be out cold." Jonas sighed. "Well, I guess we have to call the po'lice. Again." He checked his watch. "We get to Winnemucca soon. I 'spect the conductor can telegraph from there."

"We should do that right away. I have an idea who it might be, and I don't want him to get off beforehand," she said.

Jonas took a step back as if she were contagious. "Well, don' be tellin' me who he is. I got nothing to do wi' this. I jes' work here."

Concordia found herself squeezed into the same office, although a different conductor had taken over when Mr. Gould's shift ended in Salt Lake City. This man, Mr. Cameron, was not the kindly type. He squinted his already-narrow eyes as she recounted what happened and who she thought was responsible.

"I've sent a telegram to the Reno Police," he said, tugging on his tunic. "They will be waiting for us. The towns in between are too small to handle a murder inquiry."

Concordia felt the train begin to move away from the Winnemuca station. "Wait! I want to send a telegram, too. I told you that before." It was essential that the Pinkerton Agency know, so they could alert the Secret Service that one of their operatives was dead.

The conductor's stern brows lowered. "You may tell me all you like, young lady, but you are the prime suspect, and I'm not giving you the chance to communicate with any confederates you may have."

"A suspect!" Concordia cried. "That is absurd."

"Is it?" the conductor answered. "You were discovered with the body. The man in question is one whom you argued with, only hours before. A fair number of passengers witnessed the altercation in the dining car." His lip curled. "You made quite a spectacle of yourself, I hear."

Concordia felt a chill in the pit of her stomach. This had to be a joke. "As I told you, it was most likely the card sharp, Ronald Diehle, who is responsible. He and Mr. Tabor had formed an alliance – my friend Miss Hamilton saw them meeting covertly. Something must have gone wrong between them."

"You have no evidence of any sort of collusion between the victim and Mr. Diehle," Cameron retorted. "I will not smear a man's good reputation based on female conjecture. I'm aware that Mr. Tabor was a Secret Service man." He pulled out Tabor's badge and looked at it again before setting aside the wallet. "Which makes your theory even more absurd. Would such a man, highly trained in dealing with the criminal element, allow himself to be stabbed from behind by someone he'd fallen out with?" The conductor leaned closer to Concordia. The crumbs of his hastily finished breakfast lingered upon the craggy mustache. "But a woman – ah, that is a different story. How easy it would be for such a one to surprise a man unawares. One swift stroke and it is done."

"How did I lock the door from the other side? How did I come to injure my head?" Concordia snapped. She could not believe this was happening. She should not even be here. The Pinkerton office had already told her to go home. Why hadn't she listened?

The conductor turned to leave. "Locks can be manipulated. One good slam in the wind – or by a deliberate hand – is enough to jostle the latch to lock. As for the injury to your head, perhaps you did faint, from the shock of having killed a man. I don't doubt that you have little stomach for it."

News of Tabor's death circulated quickly through the train, and a worried Bill Carter came looking for Concordia. He was outraged to find her confined in the hot, airless compartment of the conductor's office, and even more outraged to learn she was detained as the murder suspect.

"This is ridiculous!" Carter exclaimed. "Miss Wells is incapable of such an act." He gestured in her direction. "How could someone of her small stature possibly plunge a knife into a man's back? Mr. Tabor was quite a tall man."

The conductor stubbornly folded his arms. "We'll see what the police think."

"But it's another five hours before we reach Reno," Carter said. "Can she at least wait in Miss Walsh's private compartment? The two women are acquaintances."

Mr. Cameron hesitated.

"She should not be locked in this tiny room. What if she swoons? And consider the propriety of the situation," Carter added. "She should not be confined, with you, unaccompanied. There is certainly no room in here for a chaperone. What would your supervisor say?"

Concordia folded her hands primly and glared at the conductor, who paled. "Very well," he said grudgingly. "But you, young lady, are not to leave Miss Walsh's compartment, or speak with anyone else."

She gave a stiff nod. How dare he treat her like a criminal, when the real murderer walked around freely? If Penelope were here, the conductor would not dare behave in such a manner.

But Penelope was *not* here, and wishing otherwise did not help. She would have to rely upon her own resources.

The conductor consulted his watch and called down the corridor. "George!" A porter hustled over, still clutching his polishing cloth. "Escort this... lady, and see that she reaches Miss Walsh's compartment. Without any detours," he added sternly.

"Yessir." The porter gave her a curious glance and led the way, although Concordia and Mr. Carter knew where they were going.

Nell appeared even more peaked than the night before. Concordia hesitated in the doorway after the porter left. "You are not well. I shouldn't impose."

Nell nodded. "I'm afraid my headache has returned—"

"May I have a minute?" Carter asked. He took Nell aside and talked in quiet tones. Nell glanced over at Concordia briefly in alarm, then back at Carter as he continued.

Finally, she reached over to Concordia and clasped her hands. "Oh my dear. I am so sorry. What a horrible experience! Please, be comfortable."

"But your headache—" Concordia began.

"It is no matter," Nell said briskly. "I have taken a powder, and should be feeling better soon."

"Can I get you anything, Miss Wells?" Carter asked.

"Could you have Jonas fetch my knitting bag?" she asked. Although she did not knit, the logbook was in there and she wanted to keep it safe. "Discreetly, of course."

After Carter had left, Nell sat down beside her. "Who do you believe killed him?" Nell asked.

Concordia's mouth set in a grim line. "I'm sure it was Roaring Ronald." She went on to describe the entries in Penelope's logbook, recording the occasions when Tabor and Ronald had been in close conversation. She left out the crossword puzzle clue and the safe-deposit box key, sensing it was best to withhold some information.

Just as Penelope would have done. She smiled to herself.

She went on to describe what happened.

Nell's face had paled during her account and she was silent for several minutes. "You're sure it was Ronald?" she asked at last. "You saw him there?"

Concordia shook her head. "It was too dark. The man is certainly small enough to hide behind one of the high-backed wing chairs, however. Considering how dangerous he is–" she gestured at Nell's scarred arm "–and the fact that they were working together, it seems credible that some disagreement arose, and Ronald decided to terminate the alliance."

Nell nodded, relief crossing her face. "I had begun to feel foolish, hiding from him all this time, but now I'm glad I took the precaution."

Concordia gave her a tired smile. "As am I."

Chapter 25

Saturday, July 16, 1898
Reno, Nevada

I t was the lunch hour when the train pulled into the station in Reno. Concordia ate little, and waited with dread for the knock upon the door. They were hauling her away to a police station in this unfamiliar town, without a friend in the world to speak up for her. How long would she be detained? What would her mother say? What would David say?

Nell and Bill Carter exchanged worried glances. "I am sure this will be cleared up," Nell said soothingly. "I would stay here with you if I could, but–"

"I know," Concordia said. "You have that interview. I remember. Thank you all the same. You both have been quite kind."

"Do write to me, in care of Bill." Nell scribbled down the address and passed it to her. "He will be sending on my correspondence, wherever I am."

The knock came at last, and Carter opened the door. A short, squat man in uniform tipped his hat and leaned in. "Lieutenant McGee, sir. Is there a Miss Concordia Wells here?"

Concordia stood and picked up the knitting bag. "I'm ready to go."

The lieutenant raised a shaggy eyebrow as she said her goodbyes.

"Good luck. Remember – write to me of what's happened." Nell gave her a quick hug.

Concordia followed the policeman down the corridor, hurrying to keep up with his rapid, waddling strides.

As they passed through several cars, she realized they were not getting off the train. In fact, they were heading for the library car.

"What is going on?" she asked.

The lieutenant held the compartment door open. "I've had orders to proceed with you to San Francisco. We can talk in here – the compartment has been closed to passengers until then."

She paused in the doorway, nervously clutching Penelope's knitting bag to her chest. "Where is... Mr. Tabor?" Surely, they would not leave the body in a hot compartment?

The man smiled. "Don't worry, miss. The body is now in our morgue. All done quite discreetly, of course. The passengers know there has been a death, but only a handful of people know any of the unpleasant particulars. The coroner will make his examination and communicate his findings to the police in San Francisco. Now, why don't you have a seat and make yourself comfortable."

"Am I under arrest?" she asked.

"Not if you cooperate," he answered easily.

She smiled stiffly and perched on the edge of the chair. "And what will my *cooperation* entail?"

The policeman checked off the list with his fingers. "One. You accompany me to San Francisco, which is your intended destination, anyway, so there's no inconvenience at all, correct? We will proceed directly to the police station at City Hall for you to answer further questions." He tugged on a second finger. "Which leads me to number two. You answer all of my questions fully and honestly along the way, without evasions." His eye strayed to the bag over her arm. "Three. You allow me to search your belongings. Now, that's not so onerous a list, is it, miss? Only what a civic-minded young lady would be willing to do, in order to solve an unfortunate murder."

Concordia grimaced. It seemed onerous enough. A trip to the police station in a strange city, probing questions, and a search of her belongings? What was she, a sneak thief? *Mercy.*

"Why do the San Francisco police wish to question me?" she asked. "The murder is not in their jurisdiction."

"I was informed that someone in particular has questions for you there. I know nothing else," McGee said. He reached for her bag. "May I?"

Realizing she had no choice, she passed it over. "What do you hope to find? A matching set of knives? A written confession?"

"Certainly that would simplify my job," he said, carefully removing items and setting them aside. He shook the now-empty bag, probing the lining.

She gritted her teeth. Sarcasm was wasted upon the man.

"Tell me about last night," McGee said, holding the bag to the light. "Everything that you remember, start to finish."

With a sigh, and knowing that this would not be the last time, she recounted going to the library for a book and some fresh air on the deck. She described groping through the compartment in the dim light and discovering the body of Algernon Tabor on the platform, face down with a knife in his back.

"I suppose I fainted after that, because I awoke on the floor. I must have hit my head on the way down." She put a hand to the side of her head.

McGee leaned over. "If you'll permit me?" His touch was gentle on her scalp as he examined the bump. "Probably the railing. How does it feel?"

"It doesn't hurt any more. Just a small lump," Concordia said.

"And when you awoke, the door from the viewing deck was locked?"

"Yes," she said.

His expression was neutral.

Did he believe her, or did he share the conductor's opinion of her guilt?

McGee turned his attention to the contents of the bag, spread out upon the side table. "Ah, a journal. Yours?"

"No, my friend's. Penelope Hamilton. She disappeared early yesterday morning. Did anyone tell you about that?"

McGee's face clouded over. "Yes. No word on the lady, I'm afraid." He opened the book, frowning over the entries.

Just as she hoped he would dismiss the cryptic notations as womanly nonsense, he set the book on his lap and regarded her with wide eyes. "Your friend is a *detective?* Are you a detective, too?"

She flushed. "Of course not. Detectives do not faint at the sight of a body."

A small smile tugged at his lips. "Many of my associates would like to think that was so. But you didn't answer my question about Miss Hamilton."

She hesitated.

"If it makes any difference, miss," he said quietly, "I do believe you are innocent of this crime. Your friend is certainly not a suspect. She was not even aboard when Mr. Tabor was killed. But, if we're going to find his murderer, I need the whole story about the two of you. It's urgent that we find your friend as well. She was working on a case that involved the murdered man, am I right? And that man was an agent for the Secret Service."

She decided to take the plunge. "It's a long story."

The lieutenant pulled out his notepad and pen. "Those are the most interesting kind."

Chapter 26

Saturday, July 16, 1898
En route to San Francisco, California

They were only a few hours away from San Francisco. Lieutenant McGee found Conductor Cameron and pulled him aside. "Miss Wells is not to be restricted or otherwise harassed, do you understand me? She is a witness, not a suspect, and is my responsibility. Now, I want to examine Mr. Tabor's belongings. Then you will come with me to Ronald Diehle's compartment. I have some questions for the fellow."

Concordia had returned to her seat to pack up her belongings and Penelope's. She stacked the cases neatly for the porter to take when he was ready, and settled in to compose a note to Nell, to let her know that she was traveling on to San Francisco after all. She hoped the lady's headache was gone.

"Hullo, miss!" an enthusiastic voice cried. It was Lian.

Concordia smiled and patted the seat beside her. "How are you? Excited to be almost home?"

The girl sat next to her, then frowned. "Heard you in trouble. Conductor very angry. But you all right now?"

Concordia sighed. "I hope so. But don't *you* worry, dear."

Lian smiled and pulled a paper flower from her pocket. "I make another *zhezhi* for you. Make you feel better."

"It's beautiful," Concordia said, cradling it in her hands. "Thank you." She had a thought. "Would you like more paper for your folding?" She noticed the girl used scraps, probably retrieved from waste bins.

The girl's eyes widened when Concordia produced several sheets of thin, eggshell-colored stationery from beneath her writing-blotter.

"Lian!" a voice called. Her mother, watching from the aisle, held up a dress, giving instructions in rapid Chinese.

The girl hopped up from the seat with a wide grin, clutching the paper. "Thank you, miss! 'Bye."

"Goodbye." What a charming girl, Concordia thought, tucking the paper flower in her pocket.

"Miss Wells," a quiet voice murmured.

She opened her eyes to see Lieutenant McGee standing over her. The sky outside her window was shadowed in dusk and the cabin's electric lights had been switched on.

"Are we there?" she asked, sitting up straighter.

"Another hour, the conductor tells me. Shall we have tea in the library in the meantime? I can catch you up on my progress of this afternoon." He glanced down at the cases beside her. "I see you are packed. Good. Where should I instruct the porter to have your case and trunk delivered?"

"I'll be staying at the Beresford," she said, remembering her aunt's message. She looked forward to accessing her trunk. It was tedious to wear the same few outfits all this time.

His eye brightened. "Excellent! That is where I am staying as well."

She wasn't sure she believed him, but she let it pass. She gathered up Penelope's knitting bag and her own reticule. "Can you ask Jonas to deliver Miss Hamilton's belongings there, too?"

"Of course." The lieutenant gallantly held out an arm to steady her as they made their way out of the compartment.

A tea tray was awaiting them, accompanied by a cookie plate of madeleines and ginger crisps. "It was the best I could do, under the circumstances," McGee said. "They're shutting down the dining car in preparation for our arrival in San Francisco."

"The tea smells wonderful." She reached for the teapot, but McGee intervened.

"Allow me."

"What did you learn?" Concordia asked, as he passed her a cup.

McGee wiped his fingers and counted upon them again. "One. Mr. Tabor's case had been searched. Two—"

"What?" Concordia interrupted. "How do you know it was searched?"

"Well," McGee answered, "either the victim was a slovenly man who liked to jumble the contents of his suitcase and then stow it away *upside down*, or someone searched it."

"Oh."

"Two," he continued, tugging on another finger, "if we are to assume that the person who locked you out on the viewing deck with the body and left you there was the same person who murdered Tabor, then it could not have been Ronald Diehle."

She could not believe her ears. "Not Ronald Diehle?" She had been so sure.

McGee nodded. "You say it was one in the morning – or a little after – when you entered the library car, correct? Well, at that time, Ronald was in the midst of an all-night poker game in his private compartment. He has three witnesses to back up his story. It was after four this morning when the game broke up."

"What about *before* the card game? Could he have been in the library then?" she asked.

"That is a possibility," he conceded. "One of the porters straightened up the library car at eleven. Mr. Tabor was the only occupant left. He was still reading, and very much alive, the porter says. Tabor assured him that he would turn off the lights on his way out."

"I see. When did the card game start?" she asked.

"Midnight."

"Well then, Ronald must have killed Mr. Tabor between eleven and midnight."

Lieutenant McGee raised an eyebrow. "If so, that means a *second* person, not the murderer, was hiding in the library when you came in, and deliberately locked you out on the viewing deck with the dead body while you were unconscious. Who would do such a thing, and why?"

She shook her head. It made no sense. "So all we know is that Mr. Tabor was killed between eleven and one. Is there any way to know more precisely when he died? A stopped watch or something?"

The lieutenant unsuccessfully suppressed a snort. "You ladies have an over-fondness for crime stories. We have nothing so convenient at hand."

She ignored the remark. She didn't read *that* much crime fiction, although she did enjoy Mr. Doyle's stories. "So what happens when we get to San Francisco? Are you just going to let Roaring Ronald go?"

"I have no choice." McGee said. "He agreed to a search of his belongings and compartment on the spot. I found nothing more incriminating than a marked deck. No bloodstained clothing, no weapons, no correspondence to tie him to Tabor or implicate him in the counterfeit scheme that you say Miss Hamilton and Tabor were investigating. I have his address in town – he's staying at the Baldwin – along with his home address, in case we have more questions." He folded his napkin and laid it on the tray.

"What about the other passengers?"

"We have no suspects that we can legitimately detain. The rail line has supplied me with the home addresses for every passenger who was aboard at the time, should the need arise." McGee sighed. "Looks like we're at a dead end, miss."

Concordia realized that Lieutenant McGee had another reason for their talk in the library: to spare her the ignominy of a police escort off the train in view of curious eyes. They waited in the library until everyone else had disembarked. Jonas came to fetch them.

"The luggage is already on its way to your hotel," he said. "I made sure Miss Hamilton's cases were on there, too."

"Thank you," Concordia said, slipping one last coin into the upturned palm. "I'm glad to have a chance to say goodbye to you."

Jonas grinned. "It's been an int'resting time, that's fo' sure."

"I appreciate everything you've done for me – and Miss Hamilton." She choked out the last words.

Jonas's expression turned to pity. "Don' you worry now, miss. They'll find her. I bet she has a good story to tell when they do." He fished in his pocket and pulled out a bent card. "Not tryin' to be forward–" he dropped his voice to a whisper "–but if you need help, I'm staying in town with my cousin this week. He lives over his shop wi' his wife and baby."

She glanced at the card. *Isaiah Markey, barber. 1023 Market St.* "Thank you," she murmured, tucking it away.

After McGee helped her off the train, she took one last look at the large iron conveyance where so much had happened over the last few days. Trainmen were already swarming the locomotive, cleaning out the ash pan, re-loading coal in the tender, checking the couplings. She may be heading for a police station, but at least it was not on wheels, which would be a welcome relief after the constant sense of motion.

"Ready?" McGee asked, extending the crook of his arm. She took it, holding onto her hat with her other hand against the stiff bay breeze.

The skies opened up with rain just as they made a dash for the line of hackney carriages in front of the station. During the short ride, Concordia gazed out the window into the growing dusk. She had never been farther west than Chicago. San Francisco's concentration of multi-storied buildings along the Market Street thoroughfare resembled that of any big city, though its streets of Belgian cobbles were much broader than those of her native Hartford. The buildings were newer as well. She could see the famed hilly streets of the city in the distance.

They were approaching a large domed building on their right. "Here we are," the lieutenant said. "City Hall."

Though still under construction, City Hall was an imposing structure, occupying two entire city blocks. It was built in the French classical style, evident by its columned façade and two domes, the larger one sitting squarely over the main entrance.

"Impressive," Concordia said, as McGee helped her out of the vehicle.

McGee grimaced. "They've been working on it for a quarter century now. Almost finished, finally."

Though grand looking from the outside, the interior revealed evidence of shoddy work: uneven flooring, ill-drawing chimneys, and…what was that smell? She wrinkled her nose. Obviously, the sewer system was woefully inadequate.

She waited while McGee spoke with the uniformed man at the counter and handed him a thick envelope.

McGee returned with a smile. "Someone is being fetched. It should only be a few minutes." He gestured to a dusty bench. "Would you care to sit?"

Concordia shook her head.

After about fifteen minutes, a short, barrel-chested man sporting a gray mustache and mutton-chop whiskers approached. He shook hands with the lieutenant. "McGee? I'm Captain Lang." He turned to Concordia, his brows lowering in a hostile expression. "You are Miss Wells? Would you step this way, please?" Without waiting for a response, he led the way, Concordia and Lieutenant McGee following.

The man was certainly no-nonsense. Her neck prickled with unease.

The room was windowless, laid in cold white tile, with a plain wood table and mismatched chairs. She noticed a curtained alcove on the far side.

"Please sit." The captain gestured to chairs. "I've read your report," he said to McGee. "It leaves a lot unanswered."

"So Ronald Diehle *is* part of the counterfeit scheme?" she asked.

"Not just part of it, Miss Wells." Tabor said. "Diehle is in charge of the entire operation. He probably instructed Whitney to make cheap purchases with large denominations of fake bills. That way, he would get back genuine money in change, which he would then send on to Diehle."

She pursed her lips. "That's makes sense…I noticed he got money back in each transaction. I didn't understand it at the time."

Tabor gave a rueful nod. "Devilishly clever. The use of conductors and other railroad staff would ensure that phony bills are all over the country in no time. Would have made it near impossible to trace the source." He glanced at Lang. "Diehle is being watched?"

Bagdale leaned forward. "Actually, our agency is taking care of that. The captain here worried his men would be recognized. One of my operatives is watching Diehle now. He seems to be settled in his hotel room for the night. I take over in—" he pulled out his watch "—two hours."

"Good," Tabor said. "You'll want a second man with you, in case Diehle has a visitor. I want anyone who has contact with him kept under surveillance, too."

Bagdale nodded. "I'll take care of it."

"How do you come to be here ahead of us?" Concordia asked Tabor. "The last I'd heard, at least one of the coffins was bound for St. Paul."

Tabor self-consciously touched his bandage. "The coffins were still in the baggage room at the Chicago station when I regained consciousness. Fortunately, the lid had not been securely latched. I managed to slip out when the area was unattended."

"But why be so circumspect about it?" McGee asked.

Concordia wondered about that, too. She would have screamed for the police at the top of her lungs if she awoke in a coffin.

Tabor passed a weary hand over his stubbled jaw. "My credentials were gone. Stolen by my attacker, I presumed. It would have taken more time than I could afford to convince the local officials of my identity. This was an inside job, and I did not want to tip off the man responsible, or his associates. A doctor friend of mine in Chicago patched me up and I arranged passage aboard an express mail train. Your train was delayed in Granger and then again in Reno – I did not know why until Lang here filled me in – so I managed to arrive just ahead of you."

Captain Lang groped in the envelope containing McGee's report and passed a billfold to Tabor, who opened it. Concordia caught a glimpse of the silver star she had seen before.

"Inside job?" she repeated. "I thought Roaring Ronald was behind all this."

"Diehle needed an inside man to keep him apprised of our investigation, and to assume my identity," Tabor said. "Turned out to be my own aide, back at the Treasury Office in Washington. John Robert Fenner boarded in Chicago, masquerading as me."

"The murdered man matches his description," Lang chimed in.

Concordia sat back, her mouth hanging open. *Robert Fenner.* The man had blurted out his own name when she had pressed him for the identity of Penelope's contact. *John* had been the name on the inscription in his poetry book. His middle name, he'd said. "What is your middle name?" she asked Tabor.

He leaned over and opened his identification. *Algernon G. Tabor.* "Gregory."

It wasn't even the same initial, and she had *seen* the identification card. In her distress over Penelope's disappearance, she had missed that detail.

"Miss Hamilton was to make contact with her friend here in San Francisco – the man trying to extricate himself from this counterfeit ring. Do you know who he is?" she asked.

Tabor shook his head. "Part of the deal was that Miss Hamilton secured the family first."

"You have my promise," Tabor chimed in, "that we will search most earnestly for Penelope." The others nodded.

She fought down the breathless panic that threatened to overwhelm her. She had never before defied a public official, and had no wish to sit in a jail cell. But she did not trust them to keep their word, once they had what they wanted.

Taking a deep breath, she clenched her hands more tightly as she looked steadily at Captain Lang. "I am not withholding information. I am delaying the sharing of it. Aid in the search for Miss Hamilton, and you will have it before the bank opens Monday morning. The box is perfectly secure in the meantime. No one, friend or foe, can access it."

Chapter 29

Sunday, July 17, 1898
San Francisco

As one might expect, a jail cell is a dreary place. Two long benches spanned the sides of the stone walled cell, where six women lounged, in the most unlady-like positions. After dusting off a small section with her handkerchief, Concordia primly sat and tried to ignore them.

She felt less than composed on the inside, however. Before they had put her in the cell, the prison matron had searched her for any weapons that might be secreted upon her person. Standard procedure, she was told, but it did not make the process any less humiliating. She did not have a weapon, of course, just Penelope's knitting bag, a watch, the keys to her suitcase and trunk, and the two *zhezhi* papers Lian had given her. All were confiscated, except for the folded dove and flower. She was allowed to keep those.

Concordia exchanged only a few polite greetings with her fellow inmates, who soon gave up trying to engage her in conversation. They did not seem a bad lot, though a bit lacking in decorum and hygiene. The woman sitting closest on the bench scratched at her scalp a great deal. Her breath also reeked of raw onions.

Concordia leaned her head against the damp wall and closed her eyes. Where was Penelope Hamilton? Was she safe? How was she to find her?

Hours later, the sound of voices in the hallway roused her. She saw a familiar, slim-built young woman, accompanied by two men.

"Nell!" Concordia jumped up from her seat. Her cell companions stirred, looking curiously at these middle-of-the-night visitors.

Nell Walsh grinned and clasped Concordia's hands through the bars. "We're getting you out of here." She inclined her head toward Mr. Carter, standing beside her. "Bill got Captain Lang to understand the effect of negative publicity, should the story get out that an innocent woman tourist had been put in jail. And of course, we would make sure that story was told," she added, with a mischievous twinkle.

"Miss Walsh, would you step aside please?" the jailer said, holding up his key ring. "I need to unlock the door." Nell obligingly moved back.

"Oooh!" a voice from behind Concordia exclaimed. It was the woman with the onion breath. "Yer Nellie Walsh, the lady reporter! I heard you was comin' ta town."

Nell nodded politely as the other women in the cell crowded to the bars.

"Get back, ladies," the jailer ordered, turning the key in the lock. "Only Miss Wells is leaving, not the rest o' you."

"Miss Wells must be a celebrity friend o' hers," one lady said in a stage whisper.

"Ooh, take me, too, Miss Walsh!" another woman called out, as Concordia stepped out of the cell. "I'm a famous celeb'rty! Have I got stories I could tell *you*!" Her cell-mates tittered.

"All right now, that's enough out o' you," the jailer growled. "Settle down." Concordia followed him down the hall, gratefully leaving the tumult behind.

"Sign here, miss," he said. He passed over her belongings. "The cap'n asks that you meet him at his office tomorrow afternoon—" he checked his watch "—I mean, today – at three o'clock."

"The captain works on a Sunday?" Carter asked.

The policeman sighed. "In this job, it don't matter what the calendar says. Three o'clock, miss. Be sure to remember, or the cap'n will have my head."

Concordia nodded and briskly followed Nell and Carter. "How did you find me?" Concordia asked, after Carter helped them into the waiting hansom cab. The vehicle took off with a clatter. "We knew from your earlier note that you were proceeding to the San Francisco police station," Nell said. "I called your hotel after a couple of hours and found out that you had never checked in, although your luggage is there."

"We worried that you were still being questioned after all this time," Carter chimed in. "I have some friends in the department, so I asked around. I found out you had a dust-up with Captain Lang – who is quite the curmudgeon, I hear – and had been locked up. So I pulled some strings to get you out."

Concordia exhaled a deep breath. "I cannot thank you two enough."

Nell waved a dismissive hand. "I could not bear the thought of you being in such a place. Besides, this way I get to hear the latest news. Have they found Tabor's killer? They no longer think that you are responsible, surely?" she added anxiously.

"It's a long story. I'll tell you all about it tomorrow," Concordia said, resting a weary head against the seat cushions. "Right now, I'm ready to tumble into bed. Can you direct the driver to the Beresford Hotel?"

Nell grimaced. "When I called, they had already given away your room. They are full up."

Concordia fished out her watch. Two o'clock in the morning! She would never find lodging at this hour.

"Don't worry," Nell soothed. "You can share with me, at the Palace Hotel. I have a suite with plenty of room. We'll get your things tomorrow. If you don't mind waiting until after my morning interview, we'll go with you to get them."

Concordia gave a grateful nod. "I don't know what I would do without you, Nell."

"One more photograph with the mayor, Miss Walsh!" a man called out. "Now smile... nice and pretty."

Concordia, standing beside the french doors of the hotel's ballroom, watched as Nell posed yet again, her smile stiff with fatigue. Questions about the lady reporter's itinerary, her previous adventures, the famous people she had met — all had been asked and answered, and the press conference was winding down.

Nell had accepted such attention with grace and humor, offering witty responses to her admirers and trading caustic repartee with her critics. But Concordia noticed the effects of exhaustion and strain upon the woman's face. She knew Nell was not entirely free of worry over Roaring Ronald. After all, the man was staying in a hotel only four blocks away. Soon she would be safely out of reach, sailing for Hong Kong the day after tomorrow.

Ronald had other fish to fry, anyway. The Pinkerton Agency, the San Francisco Police Department, and the U.S. Secret Service were keeping track of his movements. Concordia had not had a chance to tell Nell about recent developments. She planned to do so during their ride to pick up her trunk. She hoped it would ease her mind.

A little boy ran up to Nell, followed by his mother.

"Is it true you can juggle?" the boy asked, holding up a trio of balls.

Nell nodded. "Certainly, young man. I learned all sorts of things in my travels." She picked up the balls and tossed them expertly in the air. "There are some skills you never forget." With a wink, she handed back the balls, then made a coin materialize from behind the boy's ear.

"Gosh, thank you, miss!" the boy exclaimed, when she gave him the coin.

Concordia shifted restlessly, eager to retrieve her luggage and a fresh change of clothes. Her percale shirtwaist and burgundy linen were in sorry need of a good cleaning. Once she had freshened up, she would visit Aunt Stella before her three o'clock appointment with Captain Lang. Concordia prayed that she was wrong, and Uncle Karl was not mixed up in this counterfeit scheme. Perhaps he had been found in the meantime, with a perfectly reasonable explanation for his disappearance. The sinking sensation in her abdomen, however, said otherwise.

She stuck her hands in her pockets, fingering the *zhezhi* Lian had made. For want of any other occupation, she pulled it out and examined the intricate folds. At least the girl now had more than wastebasket scraps to work with. Concordia could make out *Western Union Telegraph Company* along the edge of the paper flower.

Her heart beat faster. *A telegram.* Could it be?

She smoothed open the folds with trembling fingers.

RECEIVED AT: 4:05 PM

DATED: FRIDAY, JULY 15, 1898

TO: MISS CONCORDIA WELLS

I AM SAFE, BUT A DAY BEHIND YOU. CONSULT THE LONGEST CLUE IN THE CROSSWORD FOR OUR MEETING PLACE. I WILL WAIT EACH MORNING. TELL NO ONE. WILL EXPLAIN LATER. ~P.H.

Concordia groped for a chair. I AM SAFE. There was a world of relief in those words. *Penelope was alive.* She had not realized how vulnerable and isolated she'd been feeling, when she feared Penelope was gone forever. But now, she wasn't alone anymore. A giddy lightness filled her chest.

She glanced at the paper again. TELL NO ONE. Was she the only person to know? Bagdale seemed to be operating under the assumption that Penelope was still missing, and this was dated two days ago. Why the secrecy?

She re-read the telegram. *The longest clue.* At ten letters, that would be *mercantile.* The word meant little to her. Mercantile what? She had another day to figure it out, as Penelope could not be at the meeting place before Monday morning. Being a full day behind meant the train would not arrive at the station until this evening.

Perhaps she could meet her at the station?

No. The station was being watched for the lady, as were the other stations along the line. At her own insistence, no less. She sighed. She and Penelope seemed to be working at cross-purposes. How could she have known the lady would not want to be found?

"Are you all right, Miss Wells?" a polite voice asked.

She was startled to see Lieutenant McGee at her elbow. She gave him a wide smile and slipped the paper back in her pocket. "Never better. What are you doing here?"

McGee grimaced. "I've been charged with keeping you in sight. Since Captain Lang did not say anything about how I was to accomplish that, I decided it was pointless to follow you covertly. I am sure you would easily spot me, sharing an elevator or trailing down Market Street after you."

She rolled her eyes at the mental image of McGee's squat figure slinking into corners and hugging storefronts to avoid detection.

"What do you say? Shall we tour the city together?" McGee asked amiably.

"It seems I have little choice in the matter," she retorted. "I take it this monitoring will end tomorrow morning, when I give the captain the information he requires? Or would you care to accompany me on my sightseeing and shopping excursions for the duration of my stay?"

McGee bowed with a flourish. "I am at your service, miss, for as long as you require."

She clenched her jaw. She'd forgotten that he turned a deaf ear to sarcasm.

A sarcasm-impervious policeman, however, was the least of her worries. The real problem was the fact that this man would now be dogging her heels all day. It would not do to show up at Stella's door with McGee in tow. How could she evade him long enough to see her aunt?

She glanced at Nell, who was gathering up her notepad, pens, and purse. "Would you excuse me for a moment?" She hurried over to join Nell.

"Concordia!" Nell said, her face lighting up. "Ready to head to the Beresford? Bill can call a hackney."

Concordia shook her head. "There's someone I need to see. Would you mind collecting my things and keeping them in your room for the time being? I know it's an imposition—"

"Nonsense, we're happy to help," Nell cut in. "And you're welcome to share my suite for as long as I have it. Just ask for the key at the desk when you return."

Concordia made a face. "I may not return for a while. Captain Lang wants to see me this afternoon. More questioning, I imagine."

"Well, if you're not back for dinner, we shall come and rescue you," Nell said. She scowled. "Really, the liberties these policemen take!" She nodded toward the uniformed McGee, waiting on the far side of the room. "I assume he's your guard for the day?"

"I have a plan to leave him behind," Concordia said.

Nell grinned. "I look forward to hearing of your success in that regard. In fact, you said last night you had other things to tell us." She sighed. "It seems there are never enough hours in the day."

"We'll catch up at dinner," Concordia promised.

Concordia and Lieutenant McGee stepped outside. The fog that had rolled in overnight was nearly dissipated. "Where to, miss?"

She glanced at the card Jonas had given her. "1023 Market Street." She pointed to an approaching cable car, similar in appearance to the electric-propulsion streetcars she was accustomed to in Hartford. This one sported open sides, certainly welcome on such a warm day. "Do we take that one?"

McGee pointed to the far side of the street and offered his arm. "We cross the street and take one going the other way. But it's hardly necessary, if you are equal to walking. We're only two blocks from that address."

"Very well," she said, and took his arm. "How do you know so much about the area? After all, you live in Nevada and work for the Reno police."

His arm tightened as he paused for a bicyclist swerving around them. "I worked for the San Francisco police force for many years, Miss Wells. I only recently relocated to Reno."

"Why?"

He hesitated. "Let us just say that the political powers-that-be lost patience with my unwillingness to curry favor."

She gave him a sideways glance. Noting his rigid jaw and averted eyes, she framed her next question carefully. "And Captain Lang – is he willing to 'curry favor'?" Heaven help them if that was the case. She recalled the corruptive influence of the Inner Circle back in Hartford, before it was disbanded.

McGee frowned. "I do not know. From what I understand, he recently transferred from a different precinct. Folks here don't know much about him."

"I take it the problem is widespread, if you felt it necessary to move all the way to Nevada."

He cleared his throat uneasily. "It is firmly entrenched in the day-to-day workings of this police department, which answers to our less-than-scrupulous civic leaders. You must tread carefully, miss."

She considered this in silence. Perhaps this was why Penelope wanted her arrival kept secret. Did the counterfeiting scheme go beyond Roaring Ronald? She shivered.

"So, what is at 1023 Market Street?" McGee said, in a change of subject. "I seem to recall the area consists of millinery and barber shops."

"Just visiting a friend," she said. She hoped Jonas was at his cousin's shop, and could help her concoct a plan to evade the lieutenant. She suppressed a guilty pang. She liked the policeman. She did not wish to get him in trouble. He reminded her of Lieutenant Capshaw back home, although they were as different-looking as two men could possibly be, with McGee short and squat, and Capshaw tall and gaunt. Yet both men were courteous, quick-witted, and persistent. Most definitely persistent. She hoped McGee possessed the integrity of Capshaw. She thought so, but a two-day acquaintanceship was little to go on. The first Mr. Tabor had made that clear.

She spied the striped barber pole when they were half a block away. As they approached, she saw Jonas, sitting comfortably in a rocking chair just outside the door, smoking a cheroot and enjoying the morning air.

Jonas jumped up at the sight of Concordia. "Miss Wells, why, this is a mighty big surprise!" He paused, brows lowering at the policeman. "You didn' find another body, I hope?"

"Certainly not," she said, giving the chuckling McGee a sharp look. "Since you so kindly shared your address, I wanted to stop by and say hello. I'm on my way to the milliner's," she improvised.

"Well, that's real nice o' you," Jonas said, bobbing his head. "I'd introduce you to my cousin, but Ike's busy wi' customers right now." He gestured at the storefront window, through which she could see several black men waiting patiently on benches. "Why don't you come in for a glass of lemonade and meet my cousin's wife and their little 'un?" He raised a questioning eyebrow in McGee's direction.

"Jonas, you remember the lieutenant? He's escorting me around town. To make sure I'm safe," she added. She turned to McGee. "Would you mind waiting here? I would like to visit with Jonas and his family in private."

McGee gave her a dubious frown.

"Ike can give you a haircut and a shave, and wax that fine m'stache of yours," Jonas suggested. "On the house."

McGee stroked his chin thoughtfully. "I suppose that would be all right."

The patrons sat up straighter as Concordia entered, and exchanged courteous nods. She noticed McGee eyeing the possible exits she might slip through. Unfortunately for her purposes, the apartment above the shop was only accessible by the front stairs, easily visible from the two barber chairs. Even the fire escape outside could be seen through the plate-glass window. How could she slip away?

After Jonas whispered a few words to his cousin – who gave a distracted nod and barely glanced up from shaving a client's scalp, the policeman was settled into the other chair.

"Thank you," Concordia murmured, as she followed Jonas up the creaky wooden stairs. She rummaged in her purse. "I'd be happy to pay your cousin for his services on the lieutenant's behalf."

Jonas waved her money aside. "With the po'lice, free is what he us'ully does. It's easier to have them on our side." He gave her a close look. "But you didn' come to see Mandy and her baby, or buy a hat, did you?"

She shook her head. "I need help."

She was introduced to Mandy, a petite dark-skinned woman in her early twenties, who proudly led them over to gaze upon the sleeping baby in his bassinet. "So sweet," Concordia murmured, feeling an odd pang as she watched the mother tenderly stroke her baby's fluffy dark head. *Land sakes*, she was getting sentimental.

Mandy nodded. "Someday, he grow up to help his daddy in the shop." She straightened. "Please, come sit an' have something to drink. You mus' be parched."

The kitchen area was tiny but spotless, and contained the essentials for a small family: a single-burner coal stove, sink, pantry, and even an ice box. Once they were seated around a well-worn card table in the kitchen sipping their lemonade, Concordia broached the subject. "The policeman downstairs is supposed to accompany me all day. However, I need to leave him behind, to visit someone. Do you have any ideas?"

Jonas and Mandy exchanged a worried glance.

"McGee is a good man," Concordia added hastily. "He might be a bit irritated that you helped, but he won't bring more police down upon you. You're not helping me do anything illegal. I promise. Is there any other way out of here, besides the front stairs and the fire escape?"

Jonas shook his head at first, then hesitated. "I have an idea that jes' might work."

⊚⊚

Jonas came down the staircase carrying a brimming glass. "Mandy sent me wi' a cool glass of lemonade for the nice po'liceman," he said to Ike. McGee, leaning back in the chair and his face partially lathered, gave the beverage an appreciative look.

"How kind," McGee said. "Is Miss Wells ready to go?"

"Too busy *oohing* and *ahhing* over the baby," Jonas said. He grinned and rolled his eyes. "You know women folk."

"Ah, indeed," McGee said, settling back in his chair.

Ike gestured to a side table. "Jes' set it down there. Almost finished."

Jonas did so, leaning in to whisper in his cousin's ear. The man grunted, then inched the swivel chair slightly away from the window as he made a final pass at McGee's whiskers. He reached for a warm, damp towel and wrapped it snugly around the man's face. The lieutenant sighed and closed his eyes.

Jonas signaled to Concordia, who quietly slipped down the fire escape. She gave a final wave to Jonas through the window. All the men in the shop – except for the face-swaddled McGee – cheerfully waved back at her as she hurried out of sight.

She walked briskly down Market to the Sutter Street rail line, and took the street car until she was three blocks away from Gough Street, where her aunt lived. Thank heaven she'd had the forethought to inquire directions of the desk clerk that morning.

She checked often over her shoulder. No sign of McGee. Even so, she had the uneasy feeling of being watched. Perhaps a guilty conscience was playing tricks on her.

Finally, she knocked upon her aunt's door, which was opened by a young maid. "Yes, miss?"

Concordia pulled out her card. "Does Estella Brandt live here? I'm her niece."

The girl started to smile, then took a cautious step back. "You had the measles as a child, didn' ya?"

"Yes. Aunt Stella told me about that. Poor girls. How are they recovering?" she asked, as the girl opened the door wider to let her in.

The maid rolled her eyes. "The spots are starting to fade. But the girls are runnin' us ragged–" she sucked in a breath as a small, nightgowned child peeked around the corner to watch. "Gracie ANN, you get back in your bed this instant!" The child was gone in a flash.

"I see what you mean," Concordia said. "Where's Stella?"

"Miz Brandt's taking a rest. She's plumb wore out, tending to 'em night after night. I'm the day help." She gave a little bob. "Jenny."

"Pleased to meet you, Jenny. Don't wake her just yet," Concordia said. "I can wait a bit."

The girl nodded. "Would you mind sittin' with them for a few minutes? I'm heating up their broth."

"Of course."

Jenny pointed to a long hallway and Concordia followed the sound of giggling to the girls' room.

"Who are you?" they asked, sitting upright.

"I'm your cousin, Concordia." She smiled. "Your mother and my mother are sisters."

"Oh, yes!" the older girl said. "Mamma has told us about you and Aunt...Letitia, and that you live very far away." She shifted to make room on her bed for Concordia to sit. "I'm Sara, and that's Gracie," she added.

The ten-year-old Sara looked very much like Concordia had at that age, with bright green eyes and a pale, freckled complexion, though perhaps some of the freckles were actually fading measles spots. Concordia noticed that the girl's hair was the same unfortunate shade of red, neatly brushed into two smooth braids.

"Are you here to sthee us 'cauth we're sthick?" Gracie said, talking around her thumb. The rosy-cheeked four-year-old had her mother's wide eyes of china blue and her soft blond hair, which was coming out of its raggedy braids. She scooched over to peer more closely at the visitor.

Concordia shook her head. "That's only a coincidence. It took me five days to get here from Hartford. You probably were not even ill yet." She pulled out the ribbon she had purchased in

Chicago. "I have brought you each a present." The girls squealed in delight as she tied the bows into their hair.

After a time, the conversation lagged. Sara sighed and flopped against the pillows. "I'm bored. I wish we could go outside and play."

Concordia rummaged in the toy chest in the corner and held up a wooden puzzle and a deck of cards. "Gracie, why don't you show me how well you can put this puzzle together, while Sara and I play Old Maid. Okay?"

Gracie gave a pout. "I only do puzzles with *Papa!*" She proceeded to wail. Concordia ineffectually tried to shush her. *Oh, bother.* She thought her students were loud, but those young ladies didn't come close to the volume currently emerging from this small mouth.

Jenny came running in. "What's the fuss about? Is this any way to treat our guest?" she chided the girls.

Sara put her arms protectively around Gracie. "She's sad about Papa."

As Sara quieted her sister, Concordia followed Jenny into the hall. "How long has Karl been gone?"

The girl frowned. "A week. Just before the girls got sick. Miz Brandt is out of her mind with worry."

Concordia sighed as she checked her watch. Only three hours before she was supposed to see Captain Lang. "I think it's time to wake my aunt."

Although Concordia had not seen Aunt Stella in more than a decade, there was no mistaking her. She resembled Concordia's mother in many ways: the slender build, the heart-shaped face, the pale blond hair and blue eyes. At the moment, the younger sister appeared the older of the two. Her eyes were deeply hollowed, her jawline sagged, and her shoulders slumped.

Stella's weary eyes brightened when she saw Concordia, and she clasped her hands warmly. "Oh, my dear, it has been too long! I remember you as a freckle-faced girl in a pinafore and flaming-red braids. Much like my own Sara." She took a step back and looked her up and down. "You have certainly grown up to be a lovely woman. And I hear you are to be married! When is the happy occasion to be?" She hesitated. "Or did Letitia already tell me? With all I've had to worry about lately, it's difficult remembering what day of the week it is."

"Actually, the date has not yet been decided," Concordia said.

Her aunt made a *tsk*ing sound. "Do not wait too long. You aren't getting any younger, dear."

Concordia bit off a retort.

"But where are my manners?" Stella exclaimed. "Please, sit. I am so sorry you cannot stay here with us, after coming all this way. I make a poor hostess these days." She tapped a forefinger to her chin. "I reserved hotel accommodations for you, I'm sure I did...oh dear, I hope I remembered...."

"Yes, at the Beresford. I haven't actually been there, but that's a long story," Concordia said impatiently. She leaned forward and looked searchingly in her aunt's face. "Let us dispense with the niceties. We don't have much time. I have a good idea of what Karl has been up to, and why he's gone. I can help you, but you must tell me everything you know."

It took much longer than she had anticipated to extract the story from her aunt. In order to convince Stella to reveal what she knew, Concordia was obliged to share the long story of what had already occurred at her end. This involved dealing with her aunt's disbelief that such a thing as a lady Pinkerton detective even existed, that this person was in fact a friend of Concordia's, and that such a woman had involved her in "skullduggery."

"My dear, what would your mother say?" Stella exclaimed at one point.

Concordia sighed. "Mother is the one who sent me. She wants you and the girls to return with me to Hartford. After we talk, I want you to start packing. The girls should be well enough to travel in a day or two. First, I must know. Is Karl involved in Ronald Diehle's counterfeiting operation?"

Stella gaze dropped down to her hands. "I don't know who hired Karl."

"But he *is* involved?" Concordia prompted.

Stella's eyes brimmed with tears. "Over the past couple of months, Karl had been working longer hours than was usual. Then I discovered he'd paid off our credit accounts at the grocer's and dry goods store."

"What did you do?" Concordia asked.

Her aunt flushed. "I'm ashamed to admit it, but I searched his shop and found a discarded etched plate he'd practiced on. I was afraid it was something like that. He had served time in prison, you see. Forgery. Before we were married. He promised he had left that life behind forever."

Concordia sat back in astonishment. "So he's the one who actually *makes* the plates to print the counterfeit bills?"

Stella gave a miserable nod. "He is an engraver and jeweler by trade, and quite skilled."

"Did you confront him with what you found?" Concordia asked.

Stella sighed. "He was already regretting his mistake, but didn't know how to extricate himself. Then he remembered a friend who might be able to help. Is that the lady you were talking about...Miss–"

"–Hamilton," Concordia said. "Yes. He wrote her and sent the key to a safe-deposit box. Do you know what's in it?"

She shrugged. "Some sort of evidence. I don't know."

"But that will implicate him as well," Concordia said.

Stella dabbed at her eyes with her handkerchief. "He knows he's already going back to prison. He was worried about us. The man who hired him – your Ronald Diehle, I suppose – threatened to hurt us if he didn't continue making plates. Karl saw no end to it." She gazed at Concordia, her eyes bright with hope. "But if he testifies and produces the evidence the government needs to prosecute the others, they may reduce his sentence, don't you think?"

"I don't know. I hope so," Concordia said carefully. Maybe Penelope could put in a good word for Karl. Once she made an appearance, that is. "Where is Uncle Karl now?"

"I have no idea. He's disappeared. I'm afraid to go to the police. I don't know if he's hiding, or Ronald and his men are holding him somewhere, or–" she choked on the words "– they've killed him."

"We must keep faith," Concordia said, reaching over to pat Stella's hand. "Would you recognize the man Karl was working for, or any of his associates?"

The lady shook her head. "I've never seen them. I do have the feeling we're being watched, though. Whenever I go to the market, there's always a youth loitering about, keeping the same distance behind me. A different youth each time, for the past week."

"That might be a good sign," Concordia said. "If Karl has evaded these men, they may be watching you and the house, waiting for him to make contact."

"Which he won't," Stella said miserably. "He would know how dangerous that is."

"If he's in hiding, where would he go?" Concordia asked. "He has been waiting for Miss Hamilton to arrive in town, and must have arranged to meet her–" She paused.

"What is it?" Stella asked.

"Does the word *mercantile* hold any significance for you or Karl?" Concordia asked. It was a long shot.

To her astonishment, Stella leaned forward in excitement. "Indeed it does."

It was two-thirty before Concordia left her aunt's house. "Only pack what's absolutely necessary," were her final instructions. "I hope to get us on the train the day after tomorrow. Keep the door locked."

McGee chuckled. "I'm sure that's a story worth waiting for. If you have further need of me – you know, to carry your shopping parcels–" he winked "–I'll be at the Beresford through Tuesday morning. Then I return home. I've been away from Reno long enough." He pulled out a card as they approached the revolving doors to the hotel. "Here is my home address. Write me any time."

"Thank you." Concordia read the card. *D. McGee.* "What does the *D* stand for?"

McGee blushed to the roots of his hair. "Promise you won't laugh?"

She nodded.

He cleared his throat. "Darcy."

Concordia suppressed a smile. "Your mother was a devotee of Miss Austen?"

He grinned. "Indeed she was, bless her soul."

"Will you help the police and Secret Service capture Ronald Diehle at the bank tomorrow?" she asked.

McGee shrugged. "I will ask to accompany them, certainly. I'm curious as to the contents of the box. However, it isn't my case. My job was to collect witness testimony aboard the *Overland* after Fenner's murder and escort you to Captain Lang." He gave her a stern look. "Meanwhile, miss, it is best if you stay out of this business. Don't go near the bank tomorrow. Let them handle it. We don't want you to end up like Fenner."

She shivered. She had no intention of ending up with a knife in her back. Besides, she would be heading for the Mercantile Library tomorrow morning to meet Penelope, and far from any trouble. "So you now think as I do, that Ronald Diehle killed Fenner?"

"We don't have proof, but yes, I have come around to your way of thinking." He tugged on a pudgy finger. "One. The coroner in Reno telegraphed an abbreviated report earlier this afternoon, saying the knife was plunged in the man's back with a great deal of force, begging your pardon, miss. Which means it was a man." He pulled on another finger. "Two. Roaring Ronald is handy with a knife, I hear. Three. He and Fenner were in cahoots. They could have had a falling-out. Perhaps Fenner wanted money in exchange for the key pouch you had given him? Diehle would need it in order to reclaim the evidence left by Miss Hamilton's friend."

"But you told me Ronald had an alibi after midnight," she pointed out. "How did I come to be locked out on the viewing deck?"

"An associate, perhaps, hoping to delay discovery?" McGee shook his head. "It doesn't answer everything, but it makes the most sense."

"Then why don't you arrest Ronald now for the murder?"

"The Secret Service wants to capture the entire counterfeiting ring. Following Diehle can lead them to their hide-out."

Concordia felt a chill, despite the warmth of the late afternoon. Would that also lead them to Uncle Karl?

Perhaps not. She felt sure her uncle was still in hiding from Ronald and his cohorts. Otherwise, why were they watching her aunt's house? Once Ronald and his group were arrested, she could get her aunt and nieces safely back to Hartford. But what if Uncle Karl wasn't found in the meantime?

Something else troubled her, too.

McGee frowned. "You look quite pale, Miss Wells. Is something wrong?"

She hesitated. Her thoughts were taking her in an alarming direction, and she needed his help. She would have to trust him.

"Yes, something is very wrong, lieutenant, and his name is Fred Bagdale."

McGee's eyes widened. "Care to enlighten me?"

"Consider this," she said. "Miss Hamilton abruptly disappears. Even though we know she is alive, she has remained in hiding, and sent a telegram only to *me*, and not to the Pinkerton Agency or the Secret Service. Why?"

McGee pulled at his mustache. "When you put it that way, I'd say Miss Hamilton doesn't trust the Pinkerton Agency, or at the very least, certain persons within it. Such as Bagdale."

Concordia nodded. "Exactly. This is a man who has been placed in a position of trust and considerable responsibility.

Bagdale is helping Captain Lang set the trap at the bank tomorrow. He's also in charge of monitoring Ronald Diehle's whereabouts." She caught her breath. Without proper oversight of Roaring Ronald, Nellie Walsh could be in danger, too.

McGee scowled. "I will speak with Agent Tabor, and suggest that his own men watch Diehle, just in case."

"Will Captain Lang be part of that conversation?" she asked.

McGee hesitated. "That's up to Tabor to decide. It's his operation."

"But you promise to speak with Mr. Tabor about it?"

He gave a little bow. "You can count upon me."

She breathed a sigh of relief.

"I must be going," McGee said, checking his watch. "Goodbye, Miss Wells, and safe travels back."

"Goodbye." She watched McGee's short, waddling form walk down the block before she entered the lobby.

She stopped at the front desk, and found that Nell's key was waiting for her. "Miss Walsh is out?"

The clerk nodded.

"What room is Mr. Carter in? William Carter." She had been too tired the night before to notice.

The clerk checked the register. "He's in 322, just across the hall from Miss Walsh."

She stopped at 322 on her way to Nell's suite. Carter opened the door, his face lighting up. "Miss Wells. So nice to see you." He hastily set aside his pipe when Concordia began to cough. "I do beg your pardon."

"No matter," she said. Her father had smoked a pipe, but the tobacco he used did not have the harsh smell of Mr. Carter's blend.

"We have your luggage, safe and sound. It's in Nell's room."

"Thank you." It would be a relief to change into fresh clothes. "When does Nell return? Why aren't you with her?"

His forehead creased at the sharp note of anxiety in her voice. He ushered her in, leaving the door open a discreet few inches. "What's wrong?"

She told him of her suspicions concerning Bagdale.

"You can't be sure of that," Carter pointed out, though his deep brown eyes held a troubled look. "Miss Hamilton could have sent a telegram to the agency later."

"But Bagdale says he has received no word of Miss Hamilton." Of course, Bagdale was now aware that Penelope was alive. Concordia hoped such knowledge would not put the lady in danger.

Carter pursed his lips as he thought. "So... if Miss Hamilton *did* communicate with the agency... and Bagdale was kept in the dark about it—"

"—we can draw the same conclusion: Bagdale cannot be trusted," she finished.

"Yes, I see your point," Carter said. His eyes grew wide. "And you say that he's in charge of keeping Ronald Diehle under surveillance?"

She nodded. "Bagdale oversees the men on the other shifts, when he isn't keeping watch himself."

Carter sighed. "Nell had shopping to do. She said she'd be back in—" he pulled out his watch "— another hour, now. I hate to break the news to her. She's been so nervous lately, and getting those headaches more often. I was hoping that she would relax once we were off the train and away from Roaring Ronald."

"She does seem strained," Concordia said. "Will she be able to take on such an arduous journey? After all, a trip around the world is not something to embark upon lightly."

Carter clenched his jaw. "I already asked her that, and she is determined to go."

"Since her story on Roaring Ronald will be released in a week," Concordia said, "she may as well go. It's either travel or go into hiding."

"I could keep her safe, if she would let me," Carter said, voice hardening in exasperation.

"Well, I should freshen up," she said awkwardly. She put her hand on the door. "If anything changes, let me know."

Although worried about Nell, Concordia luxuriated in a bathroom that did not lurch and vibrate. How wonderful to bathe in total privacy again, without worrying about someone pounding on the door to use the facilities. She took her time.

It was twenty minutes before the hour when she was buttoning a fresh white shirtwaist and a soft linen skirt of sprigged celery green. It was her favorite summer outfit. She carefully unpacked the straw hat with matching green ribbon. Now she had to get her bedraggled hair under control.

She searched in her reticule for a comb. Nothing. She searched her suitcase and trunk. Drat, where was her blasted comb? She cast around the room for Nell's toiletries case. She checked Nell's trunk, which had been partly unpacked, and spied the corner of a wooden box peeking out from beneath a skirt near the bottom. Curious, she pulled it out. The box was plain but sturdy, with a sliding lid. It certainly was heavy. The faded gilt stamping read: *To Nell, from Barnum's Circus.* Obviously, a souvenir from the time the lady reporter had traveled and worked with the troupe.

When she slid the box open, she sucked in a breath. Inside was a set of five knives, their matching red-lacquer hilts sickeningly familiar.

The slot for the sixth was empty.

She closed her eyes. It couldn't be. Not Nell.

Dread plucked at her stomach. She recalled Nell's earlier words.

That summer, I was a fortuneteller, a bareback horse rider, and an assistant to a knife-thrower and a magician.

Concordia reluctantly saw the puzzle coming together. Here were the mates to the murder weapon, which was no ordinary knife as they had supposed, but a throwing-knife. In accurate hands, and sharpened to a razor's edge, such a knife could be wielded by a woman with just as much force as one thrust at close quarters by a man. Nell could have acquired the skill that summer, and retained the ability, just as she had with other tricks she had learned: juggling, prestidigitation... why not knife-throwing?

But why kill Fenner? Nell barely knew the man, although she had taken an instant dislike to him. Or had Nell merely pretended he was a stranger to her? She remembered the long look that Fenner had given Nell, upon their first meeting in the dining car.

Her thoughts were interrupted by the sound of the outer door opening, and voices.

"Just a minute, let me see if she's ready." It was Nell.

Concordia stiffened. She had a choice to make, quickly. Either hide the box where she had found it and pretend she'd never seen the knives or confront Nell with the discovery.

The footsteps were approaching the bedroom door, and yet she could not will herself to move.

There was a sharp rap on the door. "Concordia, are you decent?" Nell called.

"Just a minute!" she croaked. With trembling fingers, she closed the lid, crossed the room, and restored the box to its hiding place.

The Palace Hotel's American Dining Room was quite spacious, finished in white and gold, and illuminated by hundreds of incandescent lights. Unfortunately, this added to the heat of the room, already crowded with patrons despite its large capacity.

Nell made a face. "I'm sorry I delayed our dinner. I'd forgotten the crush at this hour!"

"No matter," Bill Carter said. He guided them to the padded velvet benches in the lobby to wait.

"You've been awfully quiet, Concordia," Nell said.

Concordia was gazing at the gilt-trimmed, coffered ceiling. She grieved for the woman she had come to consider a dear friend. How could Nell be a killer? Just an hour ago, she had feared for the woman's safety at the hands of Roaring Ronald. Now she was convinced Nell was a murderess.

How could she trust her own judgment anymore? Was no one whom they seemed to be? First the man posing as Algernon Tabor, and now Nellie Walsh.

What should she do? Call the police? No, not yet. She had to know for sure before she acted. To accuse her friend of so heinous a deed....

"Concordia?" Nell leaned in, her face creased in concern. "Bill, she's quite pale. It must be this press of people. We'd better get her back to the suite."

"I'll be all right," Concordia heard herself say. Her voice felt disembodied, as if it were coming from somewhere else.

"Nonsense," Carter said briskly, steadying her on her feet. "We'll have room service sent up."

"You do look decidedly unwell, dear," Nell said. She reached out to support her other elbow, but Concordia shrank away from her touch. Nell dropped her hand, confused.

Back at Nell's suite, Carter arranged for room service while Nell fussed over Concordia. "You really should lie down," she urged.

"I'll be fine here on the divan," Concordia said. Once she felt more steady and clear-headed, she had some questions for the lady reporter.

Nell hovered uncertainly, exchanging worried glances with Carter.

At last, the dinner trays were brought, and they settled in for a quiet meal. After a bowl of soup, Concordia felt her composure return.

Nell gave her a tentative smile. "It's good to see your color coming back. So, do you feel up to telling us about your day? Were you able to dodge Lieutenant McGee, after all?"

Concordia sat up straighter. She had a role to play, and now was not the time for sentimentality and agonizing over past poor judgment. She took a breath to steady her voice. "Yes, I left him behind in a barber shop while I went to visit my aunt."

Nell chortled with glee.

"But why go to so much trouble to leave behind the policeman for a simple family visit?" Carter asked.

"My aunt is... nervous... around police." Concordia did not intend to reveal her uncle's sordid entanglement with Ronald Diehle.

Nell laughed. "Aren't we all? Especially here, where city corruption is rampant. I'll bet the lieutenant got an earful for losing you."

"Certainly from Captain Lang, but Bagdale and Tabor didn't seem too concerned about it," Concordia said.

Nell paled. "Tabor?"

Carter started out of his chair. "How can that be? Tabor is dead." His voice sounded more raspy than usual.

"Oh!" Concordia had been too tired last night to catch them up on the turn of events, and now chance had worked in her favor. She could observe Nell's reaction to the news. "The man aboard the train whom we thought was Secret Service Agent Algernon Tabor was actually a man named John Robert Fenner," she explained. "He was Tabor's aide in Washington, but secretly worked for Ronald Diehle. Ronald – or one of his henchmen, I suspect Krebs, who doesn't seem terribly clever – thought he had killed the real agent just before we reached Chicago, and stuffed him in the coffin in the baggage car."

"So that explains the embalmed corpse," Carter said. He cast an uneasy glance at Nell, no doubt second-guessing the propriety of bringing up such a subject in mixed company.

Concordia nodded.

Nell distractedly plucked a piece of lint from her sleeve. "How macabre," she said finally.

"You don't seem terribly surprised," Concordia said. She hesitated, then plunged ahead. "In fact, upon reflection, I have the sense that you knew Fenner, from before this trip. And that you knew he wasn't Algernon Tabor all along."

Carter sucked in a startled breath and frowned at his fiancée.

Nell shook her head vehemently. "I certainly did not like the man, and there seemed to be something sketchy about him.

"Really, that isn't necessary," she interrupted. The last thing she needed for a discreet meeting with Penelope was an over-eager tour guide at her heels.

The man sighed and polished his spectacles. "I assume you are in search of the popular fiction section. That's all the ladies read nowadays."

Concordia bristled, tempted to disclose her status as a college literature professor. Succumbing to such vanity, however, would merely prolong their conversation. "Thank you," she said simply.

The man gestured to a double set of doors. "There is a very pleasant ladies' reading parlor, if you wish. Enjoy your visit, miss."

She may as well start there.

Even at this early hour, the library was bustling with patrons. Every time she saw a woman who looked like Penelope, her heart would beat faster and she would be tempted to call out. Instead, she methodically circulated through the rooms and alcoves, discreetly peering at faces, here and there pulling a book from a shelf and perusing it.

She had her nose in a book, in fact, when there was a light tap upon her shoulder. She looked up into the smiling eyes of Penelope Hamilton. In her excitement, she dropped her book and clasped her friend's hands warmly. "Oh, I was so worried about you!"

Penelope put a finger to her lips and checked over her shoulder as Concordia retrieved the book. A few patrons had glanced up in curiosity, but returned to their own occupations.

Penelope looked weary, but was as meticulously groomed as usual, attired in a navy-striped linen walking dress and a smart white straw hat with matching blue ribbon. "Let us go to one of the chess rooms, where we can speak in private," she murmured.

The chess room Penelope selected contained some of the artwork the librarian had mentioned. This seemed to be a "royal" room, where the oil portraits were those of English kings. Penelope immediately walked over to the portrait of Richard the

Third and felt around the back of the frame, careful not to disturb it.

"What on earth?" Concordia exclaimed.

Penelope grunted in satisfaction as she removed an envelope that was adhered to the back. "I worried it would no longer be here."

Concordia stared, open-mouthed. "So that was what your *Richard* clue meant."

Penelope nodded ruefully. "Terribly cryptic of me, but I feared anything I left for you might be intercepted."

"Actually, your telegram was intercepted by Mr. Fenner, so it was a wise precaution," Concordia said. "It came into my hands eventually, but only by happenstance."

Penelope frowned. "Fenner?"

"The man who posed as Tabor. He's…dead. It's a long story," she added, noting Penelope's blank look.

"One which will have to wait, I'm afraid," Penelope said. She slit the envelope and pulled out a lengthy, hand-written note.

"What's that?"

"A signed confession from my friend, Karl Brandt, in case Ronald Diehle caught up to him," Penelope said.

Concordia paled and gripped the chair. "Uncle Karl is… dead?"

"I don't know. He wrote me that he would be here every day at noon, so we shall see. I'm simply securing the document…." Penelope stopped and gaped at her. "What do you mean, *Uncle* Karl?"

"Another long story," Concordia said weakly.

"One which we do not have time to tell," a deep male voice said. In the doorway stood a middle-aged man of medium height, dressed in a threadbare jacket and dusty trousers that were once black but now looked gray.

She was not sure she would have recognized her uncle after all this time. She had not seen him since his wedding more than a dozen years ago. But his eyes widened in recognition, and he reached out his hands to her. "Concordia, what a surprise, my dear. I assume your mother sent you here?"

While it was a relief that he was unharmed, she held back from embracing him. "I cannot believe you have degraded yourself so," she said coldly. "You have placed your family in unforgivable danger. I am here to bring Stella and the girls back to Hartford, where they can be safe."

Karl sighed and dropped his hands. "That's as it should be. I will go to prison easier in my mind if I know they are secure."

"Let us dispense with the family reunion, if you please," Penelope said. "Karl, it's good to see you – still alive. I have arranged a safe house for Estella and the girls. We can get them there tonight. Concordia can then accompany them on the *Overland*, which departs at ten-forty tomorrow morning. Once they are gone, I will go with you to the local Secret Service office. It's in the U.S. Appraiser's building, not far from here." She pulled out a key hung around her neck. "We'll turn this key over to them. The safe-deposit box contains evidence the government needs, yes?"

Karl nodded. "That's where I hid the damaged twenty-dollar plate."

"Damaged? How?" Concordia asked.

"I was trying to stall for time. I knew it would be a while before you could get here," Karl said, glancing at Penelope. "We were already printing bills from it, but I made it look as if it had accidentally jammed in the press, which twisted it and made it unusable. I promised to make another. I pretended to dispose of the damaged one, but put it in a bank security box instead."

"It may not be there now," Concordia said. She explained about the plan to trap Ronald Diehle. "I don't know the exact arrangements. They may allow him to take the plate, and then arrest him."

Penelope sighed. "Their plan will fail. With Bagdale on the case, Diehle will not approach the bank. He would have been warned off."

Ah, so Bagdale was indeed a confederate of Roaring Ronald. "Is that why you disappeared from the train," Concordia asked, "and didn't communicate with the Pinkerton Agency – because you knew Bagdale was corrupt?"

Penelope nodded. "I regret I couldn't share that with you at the time. When the agency received Karl's letter at the Chicago address, my supervisor thought this was the perfect opportunity to not only break up Diehle's counterfeit operation and help Karl out of his predicament, but also flush out our corrupt operatives in San Francisco. Bagdale isn't the only one, you see. They have been under suspicion for some time. But I had to be out from under his eye to do it." She sighed. "I had not planned on being completely out of touch. We were going to work with the Secret Service to arrange my disappearance. However, I felt there was something sketchy about Tabor from the beginning. Then I overheard a late-night conversation between him and Diehle. I knew I couldn't trust him."

"As it turns out, that wasn't Algernon Tabor," Concordia said. "It was his aide posing as him." She quickly filled in Penelope on the details of the attack on the real Mr. Tabor.

"I hope to heaven that *this* Tabor can be trusted," Penelope said. "This man – Fenner – was killed? What happened?"

"It's complicated," Concordia said, thinking of Nell and the knife currently residing in her purse.

Karl glanced at his watch and shifted uneasily in his chair. "As fascinating as this is, shouldn't we get Stella and the girls to that safe house now?"

"We cannot do it in daylight," Penelope said. "I've made arrangements for tonight–"

They heard a strident female voice in the hallway outside. "Karl? Karl? Where are you?"

Concordia's eyes widened. *Aunt Stella?* What was she doing here?

Karl jumped up and ran to the door, grabbing his wife by the arm and hauling her into the room. "Will you be *quiet!*" he hissed. "What in the *Sam Hill* are you doing here?"

"Oh, *Karl,*" Stella cried, embracing him, "I have been out of my mind with worry. How could you leave, without a word to me?"

"How, indeed," he said wearily, rubbing a hand over his eyes.

"The girls have been sick, and strange men have been watching the house, and I didn't know what to do," Stella protested, "and then Concordia came, and told me about the clue her friend had left her, regarding a meeting place. I helped her figure it out," she added proudly. "Oh, I just had to see you, dear!"

Both Karl and Penelope shot black looks at Concordia as she slunk in her chair. How could she know her aunt would risk seeking out Karl? Especially when their house was being watched, and their every movement monitored? The woman had all the sense of a goose.

"We'd better leave," Penelope said. "Diehle's men could have followed her here."

Stella waved a dismissive hand. "*Pshaw.* What sort of ninny do you take me for? I made sure no one followed me."

"Nevertheless, it would be wise to get out of here," Karl said, opening the door cautiously. The women trailed after him.

Karl went on ahead to check the street, then motioned to them. "No sign of him."

Concordia let out a breath as they stepped out to the sidewalk. "Now what?"

Penelope rummaged in her purse, pulling out a room key that she handed to Concordia. "I'm staying at the Baldwin, checked in under Mrs. Penelope Wynch. You and your uncle wait for me there. I'll take Estella back to the house, and make sure everything is secure before I leave. I have a few more details to take care of before—" she broke off as a hackney coach came down Van Ness at great speed.

It pulled up abruptly in front of them. The driver, who Concordia recognized as Krebs, hopped down and opened the door before they could react. Inside was Roaring Ronald, with a night gowned little girl slumped in his arms. Karl sucked in a sharp breath.

"Dear Lord," Concordia whispered. *Gracie Ann.*

"We have a great deal to discuss, Mr. Brandt. Come join us – all of you. But quietly, please," Ronald added jovially. "We mustn't wake the child."

Chapter 31

Penelope caught Stella barely in time as she sagged to the sidewalk in a faint. Concordia felt helpless as they were all prodded into the vehicle. There were pedestrians within shouting distance, and yet the sight of little Gracie Ann in Ronald's firm grip made it impossible for them to do anything but silently enter the coach. Once they were in, the vehicle took off at a rattling pace. Concordia wedged herself against the corner so as not to tumble into Penelope's lap.

"The girl was given something to make her sleep," Ronald said calmly, glancing at the jaw-clenched Karl Brandt, who couldn't take his eyes off his little girl. "She will be fine. *If* you cooperate."

Karl passed a shaking hand over his forehead. "What do you want?"

Ronald laughed caustically. "What do I *want*? I want a loyal associate. Is that too much to ask? I pay you well, Brandt, and what do I get in return? You sabotage my plate and run to the authorities. Because of you, I have to travel across the country to manage this mess, then elude the trap set by the Secret Service. Oh yes, Bagdale warned me away from the bank. It has been quite convenient, having a private detective in my employ." He glared at Karl. "Without him, I wouldn't have known what you were up to. Unfortunately, Fred couldn't intercept the letter you wrote to this one." He jerked a thumb in Penelope's direction. "Imagine my astonishment when it turns out she's a Pinkerton, too."

"Bagdale's usefulness to you is about to expire," Penelope said tartly. "The agency has been gathering evidence against him. Even if he manages to avoid prison time, he will no longer hold a position of trust in law-enforcement circles."

Ronald waved a dismissive hand and shifted his grip of Gracie, who stirred in her sleep. "No matter. I'm already grooming his replacement."

Concordia glanced over at her niece. If Gracie awoke earlier than expected and started to fuss – the piercing volume of the child's cries was fresh in her mind – perhaps it would pose enough of a distraction for them to escape when the coach stopped.

"Now," Ronald went on, turning back to Karl, "we are returning to your house, where you will complete the replacement plate you started."

"But that will take me two days, at least!" Karl protested. "And the tools I need are in my shop."

"Your equipment has already been moved," Ronald answered. "And these ladies – including your two adorable children – will act as... collateral, shall we say? You will be motivated to work more quickly. When you have completed your work to my satisfaction, I will leave with the plate, to resume operations in a new locale. The women will then be released."

Concordia and Penelope exchanged skeptical looks. Roaring Ronald would not simply let them go. Concordia glanced at Karl, who did not meet her eye. He looked beaten. Was there any fight left in him?

When they approached the Brandt house, Fred Bagdale opened the front door to meet them, his thin, craggy face creased in satisfaction. "Out," he ordered roughly. He supported a revived Stella by the elbow when she began to stumble. "Everything is under control," he said to Ronald. "The maid and the other girl are locked in the basement."

"Still asleep?" Ronald asked.

Bagdale nodded. "Good. Lock the others in there, too. If any of you makes a sound," he added in a menacing tone, "you all will be tied up and gagged. Including the children. Understand?"

Bagdale grinned when he spotted Penelope Hamilton. "Ah, the elusive Miss Hamilton. A pleasure to meet you at last. I must say, you have led us a merry chase. We have been searching far and wide for you! At your friend's insistence, I might add." He cast a mocking glance at Concordia, who winced. Penelope gave him a scornful glance but said nothing as he prodded her down the stairs.

The basement was a dismal place, the air damp and cloying. Even with the brightness of midsummer out-of-doors, the narrow transom window did little to illuminate the room. Bagdale lit a lantern as Ronald laid the sleeping Gracie next to her sister on a cot that had been set up. "Make sure they stay quiet," he said to Bagdale. "I'll be upstairs with Brandt."

Bagdale waved at the women. "Sit. You're going to be here for some time. I will be nearby, so no noise." He took the lantern with him and left them in the gloom.

As soon as he was gone, Stella ran over to her girls, trying to rouse them. "They won't wake up!" she cried.

Penelope made a *shushing* gesture. "We must be quiet. It is far better not being tied up, let me assure you." Concordia heartily agreed with that, remembering her unpleasant experience last year.

Penelope approached the girls and put an ear to their chests, doing the same with the maid, Jenny, who was sleeping on a second cot. "Their breathing and heart rates seem normal. I don't think they are in any danger. Do not try to rouse them for the time being. We need to figure out an escape. Concordia, give me a boost, will you?" She pointed to the casement window.

Concordia knelt and cupped her hands. Penelope gave a grunt and hoisted herself up. With one elbow propped on the deep ledge, she tugged at the handle. The window didn't budge. Finally, she dropped back to the floor.

"That window hasn't been opened in decades," Stella said with a gloomy sigh. "Moisture has rusted the casement, Karl says. We've never bothered with it. Besides, it's too narrow for someone to fit through."

Penelope nodded toward the girls. "Not for Gracie or Sara." She surveyed the room in the dimness. "What do you keep here? Any crowbars?"

Stella shrugged. "Odds and ends, but no tools. Karl won't store them down here. The damp is bad for them. No weapons, either. Nothing we can use to defend ourselves." She began to weep.

"Penelope," Concordia said, motioning to her. She opened her reticule and pulled out Nell's knife. Penelope's face lit up at the sight, though she raised an eyebrow in mock disapproval. "Miss Wells," she said in her best school-ma'am tone, "how do you happen to carry a knife upon your person? Hardly lady-like behavior."

Concordia gave a wan smile. "It's from a set of throwing knives belonging to Nell Walsh. I saw one of these... in Mr. Fenner's back." Her smile faded as she remembered.

Penelope's eyes widened. She was silent for a moment. Concordia could see her putting all the bits together. "Nell's circus activities," she said at last, nodding. "Knife-throwing was one of them, I recollect. You believe Nell killed Mr. Fenner?"

Concordia sighed. "I took this from what remained of the set. I only discovered the box in Nell's room last night, and one was already missing. I wanted to ask your advice as to what to do. Of course, I did not anticipate consulting you under these particular circumstances."

Penelope was examining the weapon closely. "Yes, we'll have to return to the issue later. Right now we have more pressing problems."

"We should be able to chisel the window open with the knife," Concordia said.

Penelope smiled. "My thoughts exactly. See if you can find a box to stand upon."

As Concordia rummaged among the detritus of items, Penelope waved Stella over and shared their plan in low tones. "We need you to stand by the door and listen. If you hear someone coming, give us a sign. They cannot know what we're up to."

Concordia dragged over an empty wooden crate. "It sags a bit at one end where there's some rot, but it's mostly intact."

"Perfect." Penelope jumped up and set to work.

The rest of the afternoon was occupied with Penelope and Concordia taking turns with the knife when the other tired of chipping away at the rusted, rotted window frame. The work was hot and slow, as they had to make sure no sound reached Bagdale's ears. Concordia's blouse clung to her skin and her hair came loose, trailing down her back. Penelope's appearance was equally bedraggled, and the lady mopped her forehead frequently with her handkerchief.

Stella kept an ear to the basement door and her eyes on her sleeping daughters.

At one point, Stella gave a frantic wave. "Someone coming!" she whispered.

Concordia and Penelope shoved the box in the corner and quickly perched upon one of the cots, Concordia tucking the knife in her skirt pocket just in time. She began to tidy her hair.

Bagdale, accompanied by Krebs, came in carrying a tray of cold chicken, sliced bread, and a pitcher of water.

"I was saving the chicken for tonight's dinner," Stella complained. At a look from Bagdale, she closed her mouth and said nothing more.

"The children will be waking up soon," he said. "If you cannot keep them quiet, we will be forced to use more extreme methods. Understand?" Stella nodded mutely.

Bagdale squinted at the perspiring Penelope and Concordia. "Why are you sweating so much?"

Concordia tossed her head. "That is hardly a question one asks a lady. We do not *sweat*. In case you haven't noticed, the air is quite damp and stifling down here."

Bagdale grunted and set the tray down. "Remember my warning."

As soon as he left, Concordia and Penelope went back to work.

It was dark outside by the time they had finished and at last could open the window. Concordia felt a rush of excitement.

"The children are stirring," Penelope said, pointing.

"Thank heavens," Stella breathed, as Gracie struggled to sit up. She abandoned her post by the door and hurried over to the cot.

"Mama!" Gracie cried.

"*Shh, shh*," her mother soothed, "we have to be quiet." She turned to her older daughter, gently shaking the groggy girl. "Sara.... Sara.... Wake up, dear."

Sara opened her eyes and looked around in confusion. "Why are we... in the basement?"

While Stella talked to them, Concordia and Penelope swept the scrapings from the window and floor and stowed away the box. Concordia hid the knife in her pocket again. She gestured toward the sleeping Jenny. "Should we be worried that she hasn't woken up yet?"

Penelope frowned. "I don't know. They may have given her a larger dose." She leaned in and put an ear to Jenny's chest. "She's breathing normally, but her heart rate is very slow."

"Now that we have the window open," Concordia whispered, "should we send Sara through it right away?"

Penelope pursed her lips. "Bagdale is sure to bring us a dinner tray soon. We should wait."

As if on cue, they heard footsteps on the stairs, then the key turn in the lock. This time Ronald walked in, followed by Krebs carrying a tray. Gracie shrieked in terror and crouched behind her mother.

Krebs frowned at Stella. "Shut her up."

Stella hugged Gracie close and glared at the man.

Ronald gave a chuckle. "Now, now, Myron, I'm sure the child will behave. Are we all cozy down here? Just making sure none of my chickens has flown the coop."

"Where is Karl?" Stella demanded.

"Hard at work, as he should be," Ronald said. "He's making admirable progress. Must be the motivation I have provided. In the meantime, here is tea and bread. Make it count, because it will be a while before you are brought more."

"What does that mean?" Concordia asked.

Ronald simply shrugged and gestured for Krebs to set down the tray. They left, locking the door behind them once more.

Stella picked up the teapot, but Penelope stopped her. "Just a moment." She sniffed at the tea, and tasted a small amount. She grimaced. "Either it has been steeped for much too long, or they have put something in it. Best that we not take a chance."

"But the children should have something," Stella said.

Penelope nodded. "The bread should be safe, and there is water left in the pitcher from this afternoon." She passed around the bread. Concordia, her stomach rumbling, ate hers quickly. She wished she could wash it down with a good, strong cup of tea instead of tepid water.

She eyed the window as she ate. Outside, it was pitch black. She did not like the idea of sending a young girl out alone at this hour, but they had little choice. She began to scribble a note.

"I don't think anyone will return to check on us for quite a while," Penelope said, reading the note over her shoulder. "It should be safe to send Sara out now."

"Send me where?" Sara asked, gnawing on her bread slice.

Concordia finished her note, and then crouched beside her niece. "We need you to go get help, dear. None of us adults can fit through the window, and Gracie isn't old enough." She handed Sara the note. "This is for Lieutenant McGee, at the Beresford Hotel."

Sara's eyes grew wide. "By myself?" She looked at her mother.

Stella frowned. "That's a dozen blocks from here. Can she not simply run to the nearest shop and have them call the police?"

"The shops are closed by now," Concordia said. "Besides, we don't know whom to trust in the police department. Any of them could be in Ronald Diehle's employ. But I trust McGee."

After a pause, Stella gave a reluctant nod to her daughter. "The Beresford is at the corner of Bush and Stockton. You remember the tearoom where we celebrated your friend Martha's birthday? It's just across the street."

Sara brightened. "I remember the place."

Concordia and Penelope pooled their money, and Concordia passed it over. "Once you are through the window, get a cab as soon as you are able. Do not walk the entire way. It will take too long." It could be dangerous for the girl to be out on the streets after dark, unaccompanied, but she left that thought unvoiced.

"What if the cab driver won't take me?" Sara asked.

"I grant you it may be a challenge to convince him, but tell him it's an emergency and show him that you have the fare. That should do it. Once you're at the hotel, tell the desk clerk you have an urgent message for Lieutenant McGee from Miss Concordia Wells. Even if he has retired for the night, you must insist that they wake him." She gave her niece a searching look. "Got it?"

An expression of fright briefly crossed Sara's face, but she squared her shoulders. "You can depend upon me, Aunt Concordia." She tucked the money and note in her pocket.

Concordia smiled and smoothed the girl's braid over her pinafore. "I know I can."

"Ready?" Penelope asked.

Sara exhaled a deep breath. "Ready."

They dragged the box under the casement, propped the window open, and boosted the girl up. She slipped through easily, and was gone.

Concordia sighed in relief. Perhaps this would work.

"Where'th she going?" Gracie lisped around her thumb.

Stella put on a brave smile. "It's a game of hide-and-seek, dear. Sissy's going to hide from the bad men, but we can't let them know. But don't you worry. She'll be back."

Penelope was already closing the window and shoving the box into the corner. "Lump up the blankets on the cot so it appears that Sara's sleeping. Just in case they do another check." She pulled out her watch. "Now we settle down to wait."

ᔆᓂ

Sara had always longed for an adventure of her own. No watchful Mama to tell her where to go, how to dress, when to eat or sleep or do her chores. Although her heart pounded in fright to be out alone in the dark – *how strange things were, outside at night!* – she felt a heady thrill as she hurried down the block.

Not knowing the best place to get a hansom at this hour, she listened for the rattle of carriage wheels and the clop of a horse as she kept walking in the direction of the hotel.

She had barely covered two blocks when luck was with her. In front of the rectory of Trinity Church, a passenger was climbing out of a vehicle and paying the driver.

"Wait!" she called, running across the street. The men paused and gaped at the girl.

"And who might you be?" the driver demanded, pushing back a grimy tweed cap. "Where's your ma and pa, lettin' you out this time o' night?"

Sara, gasping to catch her breath, looked up into the worried eyes of the other man, white-haired and elderly. He was dressed all in black and wore a minister's collar. "What's wrong, child?" he said kindly.

"I must get to... the Beresford... Hotel... it's an... emergency," she panted.

"I ain't taking no little girl to a hotel," the driver said, climbing up the steps to his seat.

"Just a minute," the elderly man said to the driver, then turned to Sara. "I'm Reverend Lewes, pastor of this church. I have seen you before, have I not? You live around here."

Sara nodded. She pointed down Gough Street. "That way. But we're in terrible trouble, sir. I have to give the policeman at the Beresford this note." Not knowing what else to do, she thrust it at the minister.

After a glance at the paper, the man scowled. "This is indeed serious. I'm coming with you, young lady." He opened the door and helped her in, then climbed in after, calling to the cabbie, "The Beresford, driver – quickly!"

☙❧

It took no time at all for Lieutenant McGee to pack his suitcase after dinner and shake out his uniform for the morning. As much as he enjoyed seeing some of the familiar sights in the city of his birth, he would welcome the return of his usual routine back in Reno. He was an outsider here, his presence merely tolerated and often ignored. Working with Lang had been difficult, as he never knew whether the captain was corrupt like the others he'd known.

He sighed and turned down the bed covers. The trap set at the bank had proven fruitless. Ronald Diehle neither appeared nor sent a messenger to claim the contents of the box. Secret Service Agent Tabor now had the damaged plate in his possession, but could not connect it to Diehle.

McGee had kept his promise to Miss Wells, pulling Tabor aside and warning him about Bagdale's possible association with Diehle. "You should have your own men watching Diehle. Keep an eye on Bagdale, too."

Tabor had listened with a deep frown but committed to nothing. McGee hoped he would take his advice, but it was out of his hands.

McGee wished he could see Miss Wells one last time. Quite an unusual young lady, gifted with clarity and a logical mind. He was sure she was right about Fred Bagdale. A pity she wasn't a man. She would make a cunning detective.

No, in thinking about it, he was glad she was not a man. He did not generally favor red-haired, freckled women, but there was no denying the lady was appealing, in her own way. Of course, she did have a propensity for getting herself into trouble. Whoever she married would have his hands full, he was sure.

He was drifting off to sleep when the loud ring of the hotel telephone startled him awake. He lifted the receiver. "Yes?" he asked in a groggy voice.

"My apologies for the lateness of the hour, sir. There is a gentleman and a little girl here to see you. They say they have an urgent message from a Miss Concordia Wells, and insist you come with them at once."

"Huh?" McGee passed a hand across his eyes, yawning. The clerk repeated the message. "Shall I send them up?"

He jumped up, heart racing. "No, no, have them wait. I'll be right down." He dropped the receiver and reached for his uniform.

The dank basement was not a congenial place to wait. Concordia pillowed her head in her arms at the foot of Gracie's cot and tried to make herself as comfortable as she could, but her stomach twisted with worry. It felt like hours since Sara had left, but her watch had wound down and she had no idea what time it was. Who knew what misadventure had befallen the girl, walking the city streets alone. Had she found a cabbie to take her to the hotel? Was McGee even there? He said he was not leaving until tomorrow morning, but plans change. They should have considered other options, rather than risk the safety of the child.

But what other options? Sara was their only hope of getting out of here. And if the girl did not return with help, they would have to try Gracie next, in the daylight. The child was only four, but she might make it far enough to attract the attention of a shopkeeper. By that point, they would have to risk the local police.

She watched her aunt, cradling Gracie in her arms as they both slept. She could not imagine the fear and worry the woman had endured over the past few weeks. And what of Karl, forced to do Ronald's bidding while his family was held captive? Concordia had seen the love and regret in his eyes as he watched Roaring Ronald clutch little Gracie. Karl had made a grievous mistake, to be sure, but she knew he would do anything to make up for it and keep his family safe.

Would they come out of this alive? Concordia's heart ached with a sudden longing for David. What she would not give to have him here – to help, to comfort, to simply *know* the ordeal they were going through. If something happened, would he ever learn the truth?

She knew that was a selfish longing. If David were here, his life would be at risk, too. Far better for him not to be part of this. Her own choices had brought her here.

Over the years she had known David, it had not been easy for him to understand her need to involve herself in the problems of those she loved. Two months ago, it had almost broken them apart. Not that she blamed him. She'd had trouble understanding it herself. Finally, she had come to realize that it was impossible for her to sit idly by when the people she cared about were in distress. If there was something she could do, she had to act, even when the consequences threatened to be costly. Such as now.

David, naturally, found such behavior distressing and unseemly. She knew that his own need to protect her warred with her proclivity for – *hmm*, she may as well use Capshaw's term – *meddling*. It had taken a great deal of frank discussion between them before David could come to terms with that aspect of her nature and allow her to make her own decisions, free of censure.

She smiled to herself in the dark. It was a rare man who was capable of that. Suddenly Mrs. Yarrow's words sprung to mind: *You must be the exception, rather than the rule.*

Perhaps…perhaps it *was* possible.

She heard something and raised her head to listen. The tread of feet on the stairs. Stella and Penelope sat up in alarm.

"They are perfectly safe." It was the gruff voice of Ronald Diehle, who swung open the door and held up a lantern. Concordia shielded her eyes against the glare.

"I want to be sure," growled Karl Brandt, pushing past Ronald and embracing his wife, who sobbed on his shoulder.

"Well, we're all here," Penelope said briskly, casting an uneasy glance at Concordia. "Don't worry, Karl. We are managing as best as we can." She tried to shoo him out the door.

"Where's my Gracie? Ah, there you are, pumpkin." Karl kissed the top of the sleepy child's forehead. "And Sara? He probed the blankets. "Sara?"

"We'd better run for it," Penelope whispered to Concordia, but it was too late. Ronald bellowed for Krebs, who quickly blocked the doorway with his bulk.

"Where is your daughter?" Ronald yelled at Stella, who cringed. He motioned to Krebs. "Take the other child."

"No!" Stella yelled, making a grab for the wailing Gracie. Karl lunged for Krebs, but the large man knocked him to the ground and easily hefted the struggling girl in his arms.

Then little Gracie did the most effective thing she could have possibly done.

"Ugh! The kid's puking all over me," Krebs complained, dropping the girl back on the cot and reaching for his handkerchief.

Concordia and Penelope bolted out the door and sprinted up the stairs. Concordia braced herself for an assault by Fred Bagdale, whom she could hear grunting and moving around on the first floor.

But Fred Bagdale was otherwise occupied, grappling with...*Lieutenant McGee*. Concordia stopped and stared as McGee put a prompt end to the scuffle by flattening the man with a hard right.

Agent Tabor stepped out of the shadows next, giving McGee an appreciative look as he motioned three sturdy men toward the basement. He glanced down at the groaning, nose-clutching Bagdale, and bent over to snap cuffs on his wrists. "Is that how it's done in Reno, lieutenant?"

McGee winced as he flexed his hand. "More often than I care for."

"You two are a sight for sore eyes," Concordia said, trembling in relief. "Is Sara all right?"

"Right as rain. She's outside with the Reverend," McGee said.

She looked at him blankly. "Who?"

"I'll explain after we sort everyone out," McGee said.

Tabor hauled Bagdale to his feet, just as they heard heavy feet coming up the stairs. Concordia turned to see Diehle and Krebs, arms firmly pinned behind them by Tabor's men. Karl Brandt followed, trailed by Stella, Gracie, and a third policeman, propping a groggy Jenny.

"Oh, must you take him?" Stella pleaded. "It's not his fault. Ronald made him do it."

"Now, now, Stella," Karl said, holding out his hands for the cuffs, "we knew this was coming. Thank God...it's over." His voice trembled as he struggled to master his emotions.

"You can be proud of your little Sara, Mr. Brandt," McGee said. "We would never have found you otherwise. A brave young lady."

"She's safe?" Karl asked anxiously.

McGee nodded.

Karl's shoulders slumped in relief as Tabor prodded him to follow the others.

"I'll be riding with this lot in the paddy wagon," Tabor said to McGee. "You escort the ladies to the station. We need their statements." He tipped his cap to Concordia and looked at her with twinkling gray eyes. "If you'll excuse me, Miss Wells?"

Chapter 32

Tuesday, July 19, 1898
San Francisco

The police station at City Hall was becoming so familiar to Concordia that she started down the corridor to the interrogation rooms without a second thought. Lieutenant McGee stopped her. "This way, miss. There's a waiting area for witnesses. You'll each be interviewed separately."

She sank into one of the armchairs in the waiting room. At least this was a more agreeable space than the basement. Her skirts were filthy, and she was tired. *So tired.* "Where are the others?"

"Captain Lang is interviewing Miss Hamilton. That will take some time. Another man is questioning Mrs. Brandt and the girls. Can I get you some tea?" She nodded gratefully.

Finally, the sound of the door opening roused Concordia. *Mercy,* how long had she slept? A mug of tea, long gone cold, sat on the table beside her. She glanced out the window. The morning sun was coming in full force now.

"Miss Wells?" a voice said. Concordia turned to see McGee's squat figure. "The captain is ready for you."

Concordia got up stiffly from the chair and smoothed her skirts and hair, though the improvement to her appearance was dubious. "What time is it?"

He checked his watch. "Ten."

A harassed Captain Lang stood as Concordia was ushered in. "Sit," he ordered. He also waved McGee into a chair. "You may as well stay."

"So, Miss Wells," Lang said, as he stroked his graying mutton-chop whiskers, "how is it that I arrive for work this morning to find my station crowded with four men under arrest by the Secret Service, and three of the six accompanying female witnesses in various stages of hysterics? And why was a *Nevada* policeman–" he shot a glare at McGee, who met his look, unperturbed, "–called in to rescue you and the Brandts from the hands of the most ruthless counterfeiting ring we have seen in this city in decades? Why didn't you call *us*?"

Concordia quivered with exhaustion and outrage. She expelled a deep breath to keep her voice even. "Over the course of the past seven days, I have stumbled upon two bodies, feared that my missing friend was dead, been betrayed by a man posing as a Secret Service agent, been accused of that man's murder, been put in jail, and discovered that my uncle had embroiled himself in a scheme that put himself and his family in danger. Further, I find that Mr. Bagdale, your closest associate on this case, is Ronald Diehle's right-hand man. You ask *why* I did not call upon you for help? *I do not trust you*, Captain. I am sure there are more reasons than that, but I am too fatigued to think of them at the moment."

The captain sat back in astonishment. Lieutenant McGee's lips twitched in a barely-concealed smirk.

Lang stared down at his blotter for a long moment, then gave a mighty sigh. "I was assigned to this precinct specifically to repair the damage created by my predecessor. We are not all suborned, Miss Wells." He cleared his throat. "As embarrassed as I am to admit it, Bagdale had me completely fooled. I had no idea he was working for Diehle."

She was silent, gazing out the window. What was today? Ah yes, Tuesday. She sat up straighter. Tuesday! Nell would sail for Hong Kong at noon. If she said nothing, Nell would soon be out of reach, along with her knives.

"I have something to show you." Concordia said reluctantly. She took the knife from her pocket and placed it on the table. Lang had never laid eyes upon the weapon that killed Fenner, but the lieutenant had. McGee's eyes narrowed as he recognized the red lacquer knife, even nicked and dusty as it was now.

"Before I make my statement about the events of yesterday," she went on, "we have another task to perform, before it's too late. I'll explain on the way."

The carriage made it to Wharf No. 2 in record time. Captain Lang jumped out before it came to a full stop, and quickly located the purser. "Is Miss Nell Walsh aboard?" he asked.

"No passengers have boarded yet. We're still loading the cargo," the man said. He jerked a thumb toward the brick building behind him. "Most likely, she's in the passenger lounge. They'll be called soon, though."

Nell stood up in surprise when Concordia walked in. "Concordia! How wonderful to see you before I leave. Look, Bill, it's Concordia." She nudged Carter, dozing in the seat beside her.

Carter jumped up and gave a polite bow. "How kind of you to go to such trouble, Miss Wells." He frowned at the sight of the two uniformed men standing behind her. Other passengers in the lounge watched avidly. "Is something wrong?"

Nell narrowed her eyes, finally taking in the sight of Concordia's bedraggled appearance. "What happened to *you?*"

Concordia ignored both questions, her eyes blurring. She swallowed the lump in her throat before answering. "The police want to talk with you."

Captain Lang stepped forward. "We have a carriage waiting, Miss Walsh. Come along now." He reached for her elbow, but she shrugged him off.

"What is the meaning of this? I am sailing for Hong Kong. I am *not* going anywhere with you, do you understand?" She frantically turned to Carter. "Bill, do something!"

The rest of the passengers in the lounge stared open-mouthed.

"Show her, Miss Wells," Lang ordered.

Concordia pulled out the knife. "I found a set of these in your room, Nell. One was missing from its slot. They match the knife used to kill Mr. Fenner."

Nell's eyes widened. "My throwing knives," she whispered, her lips growing white. "Where did you...? How...?"

The purser came into the lounge, clipboard in hand. "We are now boarding all passengers!" he called.

At first, no one moved, riveted by the spectacle. Then people stirred, collected their belongings, and with whispers and stares, left the lounge. The purser looked inquiringly at Nell, but Lang waved him on. "She will be staying here."

"Sit down," the captain said, as Nell swayed on her feet.

Concordia sat beside her, feeling a bit unsteady herself. "Why did you do it, Nell? I would never have believed it of you."

"Hold on," Carter said, before Nell could answer, "you are accusing Nell of killing Fenner, just because one of her knives was used as the weapon? Anyone could have slipped a knife out of that box. A porter, perhaps."

"Or you," Concordia said. An idea began to take shape in her mind.

Carter took a startled step back.

"There's more to it than just the weapon," Concordia said. "Nell, tell me about Fenner. You already knew him before this trip, didn't you?"

Nell held her gaze for a long, wretched moment, then sighed. "He was one of Ronald Diehle's cronies. Yes, I knew he wasn't Tabor. I wanted to tell you, but he threatened to tell Ronald I was aboard. He said I would die a painful death at Ronald's hands." She shuddered. "But he promised to keep my secret if I went along with his pretense."

"But you didn't believe he would keep his promise," Concordia said. "So you killed him before he had the chance to betray you. With a throwing knife that you had learned to wield during your summer with the circus troupe."

Nell stiffened. "I cannot say I am sorry Fenner is dead, but you must believe me. *I didn't kill him.*" She looked at Concordia with pleading eyes. "As far as I knew, my knife box was in the bottom of my trunk in the baggage car. The set is merely a souvenir. I certainly don't keep it near at hand. In fact, I haven't seen them the entire trip, and could not even find the key to my trunk until–" she broke off, glancing at Carter.

Concordia realized she had overlooked several important details. She turned to Bill Carter. "You said something I didn't recognize the significance of at the time. It was when you sought me out in the conductor's office on board the train, and were arguing for my release. Do you remember?"

Carter shook his head, puzzled.

"You told the conductor, 'How could someone of her small stature possibly plunge a knife into a man's back?' But how did you know then that he was stabbed in the back? Those details were not generally known. Lieutenant McGee said that only a handful of people knew that Fenner was murdered, much less *how* the murder was committed. That's not something the railroad would wish to widely broadcast."

McGee regarded Bill Carter with interest now.

Carter silently shifted from one foot to the other. He shrugged. "One hears rumors. I really do not remember."

Nell plucked at Concordia's sleeve. "How could you think Bill is involved? You know that gossip runs amok on trains, despite what the officials try to suppress."

Concordia sighed. "But there's more." She turned to McGee. "You said that Fenner's suitcase had been searched, didn't you?"

He nodded.

"By the murderer, we assume?" Concordia asked.

"What has that to do with anything?" Lang asked tersely.

"Just this," she said. "A woman would not have been able to slip into Mr. Fenner's berth in the men's sleeper car and search his case that night. Not without attracting notice. It had to have been a man."

Both policemen moved closer to Carter, who glanced around uneasily.

"It also answers the question of why I was locked out on the viewing deck overnight," Concordia went on. "The murderer needed time to search Fenner's belongings, before the alarm was raised and the dead man's property was secured by the railway officials."

"Why search Fenner's case at all?" McGee asked.

Concordia turned to Nell, whose eyes brimmed with unshed tears. "*You* know." Concordia passed over her handkerchief as Nell began to sob and rub her temples. "Your headaches will not subside until the strain of this has passed. You have suspected all along that your fiancé killed him, haven't you? The heartbreak of this has made you ill." Concordia touched her gently on the arm. "Nell, you must tell us. You cannot protect him any longer."

Carter started toward her. "Nellie, it's a trap. Don't..." He broke off as Lang took a firm grip of his arm.

Nell looked at Concordia through her tears. "Bill thought that John Fenner and I were having... an affair. We *had* been romantically involved, ages ago. Long before I met Bill." She glared at Carter. "I told you it was over and done with. Why didn't you believe me? You knew of Fenner's threats. Why would I associate myself with a man who threatened to hurt me? I loved *you*."

Carter's jaw clenched. "*Loved?*" He reached for Nell's hand, but she pulled away. "You love me still, don't you, dear? You know I would do anything for you. *Anything.*"

"Is that why you killed Fenner, Mr. Carter?" Captain Lang asked, yanking him away from Nell. "To protect your fiancée? Or was it a jealous rage?"

Carter's face took on a wistful expression. "I've protected her. Always," he murmured.

"You also locked Miss Wells on the viewing deck with the body and drew the curtains to delay discovery, isn't that right?" Lang said.

Concordia patted Nell, now sobbing on her shoulder, and looked over at Carter with profound sadness. "What were you searching for in Fenner's luggage – love letters, tokens of affection from Miss Walsh, to confirm what you feared? You found nothing there, did you? Because such tokens never existed. Nell has always been faithful to you."

Perhaps too faithful, Concordia reflected. Nell must have suspected that Carter was responsible for Fenner's death, but looked the other way.

Carter folded his arms. "I have nothing more to say."

"Very well," the captain said. "I'm taking you both into custody. You, Mr. Carter, for the murder of John Robert Fenner, and you, Miss Walsh, as an accessory."

Epilogue

Tuesday, July 26, 1898
San Francisco

The platform had grown crowded, although the train wasn't due for another half hour. Concordia's nieces were getting restless, and Jenny was having difficulty keeping them still.

Penelope had come to see them off. "The Brandt house is all packed up?"

Concordia nodded. "It took nearly a week, but we're finally done."

"I understand that Estella is remaining here for Karl's trial," Penelope said.

Concordia glanced over at her nieces, then fished in her purse for some change. "Jenny, why don't you take the children over to the flavored ices stand?" The maid gave a nod and shepherded the girls out of earshot.

Penelope watched them skip excitedly over to the vendor's cart. "You'll have your hands full with those two, especially without their mother."

Concordia sighed. "At least I have Jenny to help." Thankfully, the young maid had recovered from the unpleasant experience without any lingering after-effects. "I wish you were returning with us."

Penelope shook her head. "The agency needs me to stay behind at the San Francisco office and clean up the mess Bagdale left behind. But back to Estella. She is staying for the trial?"

"She's needed as a witness," Concordia said. "And she would want to, for Karl's sake. You remember the rector of the church nearby, where Sara went for help? He has offered to let Aunt Stella share the housekeeper's quarters at the rectory for the next few weeks. She will join us in Hartford after the trial. The minister has even volunteered to visit Karl in prison regularly."

"I suppose prison for Karl is unavoidable," Penelope said. "Though the evidence he has provided the prosecutors may serve to reduce his sentence."

Concordia grimaced. "No matter what, it will be hard on the family." She raised a curious brow. "You've never told me how you know my uncle."

Penelope shrugged. "That was years ago, when I was married. My husband had a hand in putting him in prison the first time. We have kept in touch since then."

Concordia smiled to herself. Penelope certainly knew some unconventional people.

"Agent Tabor tells me they have caught the entire counterfeiting ring and shut down their operations," Penelope said. "As Tabor put it, Bagdale 'sang like a bird'."

Concordia nodded. "I've been reading about it all week. However, the papers didn't explain why an embalmed corpse had been taken out of its coffin and Mr. Tabor put in there."

Penelope chuckled. "As you had guessed, that was Myron Krebs's doing. The man is certainly a weak link in Diehle's organization. He would have proved to be Diehle's downfall eventually, I am sure. Though physically powerful and ruthless, thinking for himself and improvising at the last minute are not his strengths. I know, because Diehle sent him after me when I jumped off the train near the Cheyenne station. I eluded him easily."

Concordia shuddered. "I was so worried about you."

Penelope's frown was heavy with regret. "Sometimes this job involves putting loved ones through trying times," she said quietly.

"So Krebs has confessed to trying to murder Agent Tabor?"

Penelope nodded. "And he was responsible for the death of the first conductor – remember the man we were originally assigned to watch? The man was, in fact, in Ronald Diehle's employ. When word reached Diehle that we were investigating – a leak at the railway end, I'm told – he ordered Krebs to silence him. With that murder on top of everything else, Krebs will serve a lengthy sentence."

"But what about the attack on Mr. Tabor? How did he come to be put inside a coffin?" Concordia asked.

"Despite Tabor's precautions, they quickly discovered he was aboard. Diehle instructed Krebs to kill the agent and take his identification for Fenner to use later. Krebs thought he had killed Tabor. He had planned to dispose of the body by dumping it off the train, as he had with the first conductor, but he could not manage it. According to Krebs's statement, someone was moving around in the vestibule. Diehle had made very clear to Krebs that the body must not be found, especially since their impostor was coming aboard in Chicago the next morning. When Krebs spied the coffin, he thought to cram Tabor in there, too, but of course two bodies won't fit. Even Krebs should have known that. He removed the, *er*, previous occupant, and tried to fit that body in one of the larger trunks – mine being one of them – but could not, because embalmed bodies are stiff."

"Not *rigor mortis*," Concordia said, a twinkle in her eye.

Penelope gave a rueful shake of her head and went on. "So Krebs hid the embalmed body behind the trunk instead, put Tabor in the coffin and closed the lid. After Diehle learned what Krebs did, he had Conductor Whitney get the coffins off the train as quickly as he could, before the confusion could be cleared up and Tabor discovered in the coffin."

"So Whitney was in on that, too. It certainly created a great deal of turmoil, which worked in their favor," Concordia said.

Penelope nodded. "And now Krebs's confession, added to Karl's and Bagdale's, has stacked the deck heavily against Roaring Ronald. He won't be able to weasel out of *these* charges."

"Thank heaven for that."

They were silent for a moment. Concordia tried not to think about what could have happened in the Brandts' basement.

Judging by Penelope's expression, she was avoiding the topic as well.

"I read Nell's exposé of Roaring Ronald's extensive criminal network in today's newspaper," Penelope said.

Concordia roused herself. "Oh? I was too busy to read the morning paper."

"It is syndicated in several newspapers across the country, so you'll no doubt run across it." Penelope looked at Concordia closely. "I assume you are relieved that it was not Nell who murdered Fenner?"

Concordia nodded, though the betrayal stung. If only Nell had trusted them and revealed Fenner's identity right away. Penelope would not have been put in danger, and a great deal of this mess could have been avoided.

"But the police finally let her go, did they not?" Penelope asked.

"Yes. She sent me a note, saying she was leaving for Pittsburgh. She had already given her deposition and did not want to stay for Bill Carter's trial. She wants nothing more to do with the man." Concordia could certainly see why. It was obvious that Carter's jealousy and excessive protectiveness were signs of a mentally unbalanced mind. She touched the brooch at her throat, ever grateful for the extraordinary people in her life.

Penelope broke into her thoughts. "What about her trip around the world?"

"Postponed. She says she is not equal to it."

"Well, I hope she goes ahead with it eventually," Penelope said. "An adventure such as that can help heal a broken heart." She gave Concordia a long look. "Or help a woman make a life-changing decision."

Concordia knew she was talking about David. She smiled. "I *have* come to a decision."

They were interrupted by the return of Sara and Gracie. A harassed Jenny trailed after them with a large kerchief. "Gracie, I must wipe your face! You are still sticky, my little miss."

The platform rumbled underfoot as the locomotive came into view. Passengers started forward eagerly. For some, an adventure awaited them. For others, it was the promise of *home*. For Concordia, it was both.

"Good-bye, Penelope," she said, giving her a warm hug before reaching for Gracie's hand. She clasped it firmly and stepped toward the slowing train.

"Wait!" Penelope cried. "You haven't told me what you decided."

Concordia looked back, a mischievous gleam in her eye. "Let us just say that your attendance will soon be requested. Memorial Chapel, I expect, just after the New Year. Will you come?"

❧ THE END ❧

Afterword and Acknowledgments

It's an exciting time to be a historical author, with the wealth of digitized historical material – both text and photographs – available on the world wide web. Nineteenth century train travel has been a particularly fascinating area of research. Here are some of the resources I turned to repeatedly in the writing of this book:

Appletons' General Guide to the United States and Canada: Western and Southern states. D. Appleton and Company, 1889.

Appletons' General Guide to the United States and Canada: New England and Middle states and Canada. D. Appleton and Company, 1898.

A Brief Illustrated History of the Palace Hotel in San Francisco. www.thepalacehotel.org

Central Pacific Railroad Photographic Museum. www.cprr.org

A correct map of the United States, showing the Union Pacific, the overland route and connections. Knight, Leonard and Company, 1892.

The Pullman Era. Chicago Historical Society. www.chicagoohs.org/history/pullman.html

Rand-McNally Official Railway Guide and Hand Book. American Railway Guide Company, 1902.

Richter, Amy G. *Home on the Rails: Women, the Railroad, and the Rise of Public Domesticity.* University of North Carolina Press, 2005.

For those who wish to explore additional nineteenth century resources (particularly those used to write the Concordia Wells mysteries), I've shared some wonderful primary and secondary sources on my website, http://kbowenmysteries.com. I'd love to see you there.

I hope you enjoyed the novel. Should you feel so inclined, please consider leaving a quick review on Amazon http://www.amazon.com/K.B.-Owen/e/B00BJ34NW8/ or your favorite online book venue. Word of mouth is essential to helping readers find books they will love, particularly those written by independently published authors. Thank you!

To order other books in the Concordia Wells series, please visit: http://kbowenmysteries.com/books. Purchase links to all of the online venues are provided on that page.

Special Thanks

Many people have had a hand in making this book a reality, and I want to express my sincerest thanks to them here. Among those who helped were several experts. Please note that any errors found are solely mine, not theirs.

To **Rachel Funk Heller**, for her invaluable assistance in the early stages of constructing my story.

To beta editors **Margot Kinberg** and **Elizabeth Anne Mitchell**, for their thoughtful feedback. Your suggestions improved the book immensely.

To **Kristen Lamb**, for her critique of my opening pages.

To **Lena Corazon**, for her input regarding the novel's San Francisco scenes.

To **Renee Schuls-Jacobson**, for giving Lieutenant McGee his first name.

To **Dale Heiser**, who furnished me with crucial information for a major plot point.

To the **Central Pacific Railroad Photographic Museum**, for answering many of my questions and pointing me to important online resources.

To fellow Misterio Press authors **Kassandra Lamb** and **Vinnie Hansen,** who provided invaluable editing in the novel's final stages, and **Kirsten Weiss,** for her meticulous formatting. For the latest mysteries by these and other authors at Misterio Press, please visit: http://misteriopress.com/misterio-press-bookstore/#all.

To artist **Melinda VanLone,** who creates all of my wonderful covers. I am grateful for her time and talents. She can be reached at bookcovercorner.com.

To **Debora Lewis**, for her beautiful interior formatting of the print version.

To **Kristen Lamb, Piper Bayard,** and the generous community of fellow writers known as WANAs, for their advice and support. We are truly not alone.

To my parents-in-law, **Steve** and **Lyn Owen**, and the extended Owen clan of wonderful sisters- and brothers-in-law, nieces and nephews. You continue to read my books and cheer on my milestones. Thank you!

To my parents, **Ag** and **Steve Belin**, for their unfailing love and support.

To my sons, **Patrick, Liam, and Corey**, to whom this book is dedicated. I am so grateful for your support of my writing efforts.

Most of all, I want to thank my husband **Paul Owen** for his love and encouragement. These books would not be possible without you.

K.B. Owen

October 2015

Bruce County Public Library
1243 Mackenzie Rd.
Port Elgin ON N0H 2C6

CPSIA information can be obtained at www.ICGtesting.com
Printed in the USA
LVOW10s1807110216

474714LV00022B/575/P